WHO IS JACQ[UELINE]

After following a lone husky on the street, Paul Hewlett encounters the dog's owner — a beautiful young woman in furs, who is then savagely set upon by two strangers who attempt to abduct her. Thanks to Paul and the faithful hound, the would-be kidnappers are repelled, and he takes the mysterious woman — Jacqueline — to his apartment, leaving her there to sleep. But on returning, he discovers a grisly tableau: Jacqueline clutching a blood-stained knife, with a dead man at her feet . . .

VICTOR ROUSSEAU

WHO IS JACQUELINE?

Complete and Unabridged

LINFORD
Leicester

First published in Great Britain

First Linford Edition
published 2018

A catalogue record for this book is available
from the British Library.

ISBN 978–1–4448–3668–4

Published by
F. A. Thorpe (Publishing)
Anstey, Leicestershire

Set by Words & Graphics Ltd.
Anstey, Leicestershire
Printed and bound in Great Britain by
T. J. International Ltd., Padstow, Cornwall

This book is printed on acid-free paper

1

A Dog and a Damsel

As I sat on a bench in Madison Square after half past eleven in the evening, at the end of one of those mild days that sometimes occur in New York even at the beginning of December, a dog came trotting up to me, stopped at my feet, and whined.

There is nothing remarkable in having a strange dog run to one, nor in seeing the creature rise on its hind legs and paw at you for notice and a caress. Only, this happened to be a husky. I knew the breed, having spent a summer in Labrador.

I stroked the beast, noticing a heavy collar with the silver studs. It lay down at my feet, raising its head sometimes to whine, and sometimes darting off a little way and coming back to tug at the lower edge of my overcoat. But my mind was too much occupied for me to take any but a perfunctory interest. My eight years of thankless drudgery as a clerk, following on a brief adventurous period after I ran away to sea from my English home, had terminated three days before, upon receipt of a legacy, and I had at once left Tom Carson's employment.

Six thousand guineas — thirty thousand dollars — the will said. I had not seen my uncle since I was a boy. But he had been a bachelor, we were both Hewletts, and I had been named Paul after him.

I had seen for some time that Carson meant to get rid of me. It had been a satisfaction to me to get rid of him instead. He had been alternately a prospector and a company promoter all the working years of his rather shabby life. He had organized some dubious concerns; but his new offices on Broadway were fitted so unostentatiously that anyone could see the Northern Exploitation Company was not trying to glitter for the benefit of the small investor.

Coal fields and timberland somewhere in Canada, the concession was supposed to be. But Tom was as secretive as a clam, except with Simon Leroux. Leroux was a parish politician from some place near Quebec, and his clean-shaven, wrinkled face was as hard and mean as that of any city boss in the United States. His vile Anglo-French expletives were as nauseous as his cigars. He and old Tom used to be closeted together for hours at a time.

I never liked the man, and I never cared for Carson's business ways. I was glad to leave him the day after my legacy arrived. He only snorted when I gave him notice, and told the cashier to pay me my salary to date. He had long before summed me up as a spiritless drudge. I don't believe he gave another thought to me after I left his office.

My plans were vague. I had been occupying, at a low rental, a tiny apartment consisting of two rooms, a bath, and what is called a 'kitchenette' at the top of an old building in Tenth Street which was about to be pulled down. I had arranged to leave the next day, and a storage company was to call in the morning for my few sticks of furniture. I had considered taking boat for Jamaica. I wanted to think and plan. I had nobody dependent on me, and was resolved to invest my little fortune in such a way that I might have a modest competence, so that the dreadful spectre of poverty might never leer at me again.

The husky was growing uneasy. It would run from me, looking round with a succession of short barks, then run back and tug at my overcoat again. Evidently it wished me to accompany it, and I wondered who its master was and how it came to be there. I stooped and looked at the collar. There was no name on it, except the maker's, scratched and illegible. I rose and followed the beast, which showed its eager delight by running ahead of me, turning round at times to bark, and then continuing on its way with a precision which showed me that it was certain of its destination.

As I crossed Madison Square, the light on the Metropolitan Tower flashed the first quarter. Broadway was in full glare. The lure of electric signs winked at me from every corner. The restaurants were disgorging their patrons, and beautifully dressed women in fine furs, accompanied by escorts in evening dress, stood on the pavements. Taxicabs whirled through the slush. I began to feel a renewal in me of the thrill the city had inspired when I entered it a younger and a more hopeful man.

The dog turned down a street in the Twenties, ran on a few yards, bounded up a flight of stone steps, and began scratching at the door of a house that was apparently empty. I say apparently, because the shades were down at every window and the interior was unlit, as seen from the street. But I knew that at that hour it must contain from fifty to a hundred people.

This place I knew by reputation. It was Jim Daly's notorious but decently conducted gambling establishment, which was running full blast at a time when every other institution of this character had found it convenient to shut down. So the creature's master was inside Daly's, and it wished me to get him out. This was evidence of unusual discernment in his best friend, but it was hardly my prerogative to exercise moral supervision over this adventurous explorer of a chillier country. I looked in some disappointment at the closed doors and turned away.

I had proceeded about three paces when the lock clicked. I stopped. The front door opened cautiously, and the gray head of Jim's black butler appeared. Behind it was the famous grille of cast steel, capable, according to rumour, of defying the axes of any number of raiding reformers.

Then emerged one of the most beautiful women that I had ever seen. She could not have been more than twenty years of age. Her hair was of a fair brown, the features modelled splendidly, the head poised upon a flawless throat that gleamed white beneath a neckpiece of magnificent sable. She carried a sable muff, too, and under these furs was a dress of unstylish fashion and cut that contrasted curiously with them. In one hand she carried a bag, into which she was stuffing a large roll of bills.

As she stepped down to the street, the

dog leaped up at her. A hand fell caressingly upon the creature's head, and I knew that she had one servant who would be faithful unto death. She passed so close to me that her dress brushed my overcoat, and for an instant her eyes met mine. There was a look in them that startled me — terror and helplessness, as though she had suffered some benumbing shock which made her actions more automatic than conscious.

This was no woman of the class that one might expect to find in Daly's. There was innocence in the face, as one sees it in young girls. I was bewildered. What was a woman like that doing in Daly's at half past twelve in the morning?

She began walking slowly and seemingly aimlessly, along the street in the direction of Sixth Avenue. My curiosity aroused, I followed her at a decent interval to see what she was going to do. But she did not seem to know. She looked as if she had stepped out of a cloister into an unknown world, and the dog added to the strangeness of the picture.

The street loafers stared after her, and

two men began walking abreast of her on the other side of the road. I followed more closely. As she stood upon the curb on the east side of Sixth Avenue, I saw her glance timidly up and down before venturing to cross. There was little traffic, and the cars were running at wide intervals, but it was quite half a minute before she summoned the resolution to plunge beneath the structure of the elevated railroad. When she had reached the other side, she stood still again before continuing westward.

The two men crossed the street and planted themselves behind her. They were speaking in a tongue that sounded like French, and one had a patch over his eye. A taxicab was crawling up behind them. I was sure that they were in pursuit of her.

The four of us were almost abreast in the middle of the long block between Sixth and Seventh Avenues. We were passing a high wall, and the street was almost empty. Suddenly the man with the patch turned on me, lowered his head, and butted me off my feet. I fell into the roadway, and at that instant the second fellow grasped the woman by the arm and the taxicab whirled up and stopped.

The woman's assailants seemed to be trying to force her into the cab. One caught at her arm, the other seized her waist. The bag flew open, scattering a shower of gold pieces upon the pavement. And then, before I could rise, the dog had leaped at the throat of the man with the patch and sent him stumbling backward. Before he recovered his balance, I was at the other man, striking out right and left.

It was all the act of an instant, and in an instant the two men had jumped into the taxicab and were being driven swiftly away. I was standing beside the terrified woman, while an ill-looking crowd, gathering from God knew where, sur-rounded us and fought like harpies for the coins which lay scattered about.

I laid my hands on one who had grabbed a gold piece from between my feet, but the woman pulled at my arm distractedly. She was white and trem-bling, and her big grey eyes were full of fear. 'Help me!' she pleaded, clinging to my sleeve with her little gloved hands.

'The money is nothing. I have eight thousand dollars more in my bag. Help me away!'

She spoke in a foreign, bookish accent, as though she had learned English at school. Fortunately for us, the mob was too busily engrossed in its search to hear her words.

So I drew her arm through mine and we hurried toward Sixth Avenue, where we took an uptown car. We had reached Herald Square when it occurred to me that my companion did not seem to know her destination. So we descended there. I intended to order a taxicab for her, had forgotten the dog, but now the beautiful creature came bounding up to us.

'Where are you going?' I asked the woman. 'I will take you to your home — or hotel,' I added.

'I do not know where I am going,' she answered slowly. 'I have never been in New York until today.'

'You have friends here?' I asked. She shook her head. 'But are you really carrying eight thousand dollars about with you in New York at night?' I asked in amazement. 'Don't you know this city is full of thieves, and that you are in the worst district?'

For a moment it occurred to me that she might have been decoyed into Daly's. And yet I knew it was not that sort of place; indeed, Daly's chief desire was to remain as inconspicuous as possible. It was very difficult to get into Daly's.

'Do you know the character of the place you came out of?' I asked, trying to find some clue to her actions.

'The character? Oh, yes. That is Mr. Daly's gaming-house. I came to New York to play at roulette there.'

She was looking at me so frankly that I was sure she was wholly ignorant of evil.

'My father is too ill to play himself,' she explained, 'so I must find a hotel near Mr. Daly's house, and then I shall play every night until our fortune is made. Tonight I lost nearly two thousand dollars. But I was nervous in that strange place. And the system expressly says that one may lose at first. Tomorrow I raise the stakes and we shall begin to win. See?' She pulled a little pad from her bag

11

covered with a maze of figuring.

'But where do you come from?' I asked. 'Where is your father?'

Again I saw that look of terror come into her eyes. She glanced quickly about her, and I was sure she was thinking of escaping from me. I hastened to reassure her. 'Forgive me,' I said. 'It is no business of mine. And now, if you will trust me a little further, I will try to find a hotel for you.'

I took her to several hotels, each in turn. Vain hope! You know what the New York hotels are. When I asked for a room for her, the clerk would eye her furs dubiously, look over his book in pretense, and then inform me that the hotel was full. At the last one, I sat down in the lobby and sent her to the clerk's desk alone, but that was equally useless. I realized pretty soon that no reputable hotel in New York City would accommodate her at that hour.

We were standing presently in front of the *Herald* office. Her hand held my arm, and I was conscious of an absurd desire to keep it there as long as possible. My curiosity had given place to deep anxiety on her account. What was this child doing in New York alone, and what sort of father had let her come, if her story were true? What was she? A European? An Argentine? A runaway from some South American convent? Her skin was too fair for Spanish blood to flow beneath it. She looked French and had something of the French frankness. Canadian? I dared not ask her any more questions. There was only one thing to do.

'It is evident that you must go somewhere tonight,' I said. 'I have two rooms on Tenth Street which I am vacating tomorrow. They are poorly furnished, but there is clean linen; and if you will occupy them for the night I can go elsewhere, and I will call for you at nine in the morning.'

She smiled at me gratefully. She did not seem surprised at all.

'You have some baggage?' I asked.

'No, *monsieur*,' she answered.

She *was* French, then — Canadian-French, I had no doubt. I was hardly surprised at her answer. I had ceased to be surprised at anything she told me.

'Tomorrow I shall show you where to make some purchases, then,' I said. 'And now, *mademoiselle*, suppose we take a taxicab.'

As her hand tightened upon my arm, I saw a man standing on the west side of Broadway and staring intently at us. He was of a singular appearance. He wore a fur coat with a collar of Persian lamb, and on his head was a black lambskin cap such as is worn in colder climates, but it seldom seen in New York. He looked about thirty years of age, he had an aspect decidedly foreign, and I imagined that he was scowling at us malignantly.

I was not sure that this surmise was not due to an overactive imagination, but I was determined to get away from the man's scrutiny, so I called a taxicab and gave the driver my address. 'Go through some side streets and go fast,' I said.

The fellow nodded. He understood my motive, though I fear he may have misinterpreted the circumstances. We entered, and the woman nestled back against the comfortable cushions, and we

14

drove at a furious speed, dodging down side streets at a rate that should have defied pursuit.

During the drive, I instructed my companion emphatically. 'Since you have no friends here, you must have confidence in me, *mademoiselle*,' I said.

'And you are my friend? Well, *monsieur*, be sure I trust you,' she answered.

'Listen carefully,' I continued. 'You must not admit anybody to the apartment until I ring tomorrow. I have the key, and I shall arrive at nine and ring, and then unlock the door. But take no notice of the bell. You understand?'

'Yes, *monsieur*,' she answered wearily. Her eyelids drooped; I saw that she was very tired.

When the taxicab deposited us in front of the house, I glanced hastily up and down the road. There was another cab at the east end of the street, but I could not discern if it were approaching me or stationary. I opened the front door quickly and admitted my companion, then preceded her up the uncarpeted stairs to my little apartment on the top floor. I was the only tenant in the house, and therefore there would be no cause for embarrassment.

As I opened the door of my apartment, the dog pushed past me. Again I had forgotten it; but it had not forgotten its mistress. I looked inside my bare little rooms. It was hard to leave her.

'Till tomorrow, *mademoiselle*,' I said. 'And won't you tell me your name?'

She drew off her glove and put one hand in mine. 'Jacqueline,' she answered. 'And yours?'

'Paul,' I said.

'*Au revoir, Monsieur* Paul, then, and take my gratitude with you for your goodness.'

I let her hand fall and hurried down the stairs, confused and choking, for there was a wedding ring upon her finger.

2

Back in the Room

The situation had become more preposterous than ever. Two hours before, it would have been unimaginable; one hour ago I had merely been offering aid to a young woman in distress; now she was occupying my rooms and I was hurrying along Tenth Street, careless as to my destination, and feeling as though the whole world was crumbling about my head because she wore a wedding ring.

Certainly I was not in love with her; I hardly could be, since I had only just met her. I had been conscious only of a desire to help her, merging by degrees into pity for her friendlessness. But the wedding ring — what hopes, then, had begun to spring up in my heart? I could not fathom them; I only knew that my exaltation had given place to profound dejection.

As I passed up the street, the taxicab

which I had seen at the east end came rapidly toward me. It passed, and I stopped and looked after it. I was certain that it slackened speed outside the door of the old building, but again it went on quickly, until it was lost to view in the distance.

Had I given the pursuers a clue by my reappearance?

I watched for a few moments longer, but the vehicle did not return, and I dismissed the idea as folly. In truth, there was no reason to suppose that the man I had seen in Herald Square was connected with the two others, or that any of the three had followed us. No doubt the third man was but a street loafer of the familiar type, attracted by Jacqueline's unusual appearance.

And, after all, New York was a civilized city, and I could be sure of the woman's safety behind the street door-lock and that of my apartment door. So I declined to go back and assure myself that she was all right. I must find a hotel and get a good night's sleep. In the morning, undoubtedly, I would see the episode in a less romantic fashion.

As I went on, new thoughts began to press on my imagination. The tale about the father, the assumed ignorance of the conventions — how much could be believed? Had she not probably left her husband in some Canadian city and come to New York to enjoy her holiday in her own fashion? Could she innocently have adventured to Daly's door and actually have succeeded in gaining admission? Why, many a would-be gambler had had the wicket of the grille slammed in his face by the old butler. Perhaps she was worse than I was even now imagining!

I had turned up Fifth Avenue, and had reached Twelfth or Thirteenth Street when I thought I heard the patter of the husky's feet behind me. I spun around, startled, but there was only the long stretch of pavement, wet from a slight recent shower, and the reflection of the white arc-lights in it.

I had resumed my course when I was sure I heard the pattering again. And again I saw nothing.

A moment later I was hurrying back

toward the apartment-house. My nerves had suddenly become unstrung. I felt sure now that some imminent danger was threatening Jacqueline. I could not bear the suspense of waiting till morning. I wanted to save her from something that I felt intimately, but did not understand, and at which my reason mocked in vain.

And as I ran, I thought I heard the patter of the dog's feet, pacing mine. I was rounding the corner of Tenth Street now, and realized the folly of my behaviour. I stopped and tried to think. Was it some instinct that was taking me back, or was it the remembrance of Jacqueline's beauty? The desire to see her, to ask her about the ring?

I had actually swung around when I heard the ghostly patter of the feet again close at my side. I made my decision in that instant, and hurried swiftly on my course back toward the apartment house. I was in Tenth Street now. It was half-past two in the morning, and beginning to grow cold. The thoroughfare was empty. I fled between two rows of high, dark houses.

When at last I found my door, my hands were trembling so that I could hardly fit the key into the lock. I wondered now whether it had not been the pattering of my heart that I had heard.

I bounded up the stairs. But on the top storey I had to pause to get my breath, and I listened outside. There was no sound from within.

The two rooms that I occupied were separated only by a curtain, which fell short a foot from the floor and was slung on a wooden pole, disclosing two feet between the top of it and the ceiling. The rooms were thus actually one, and the bed in the rear room was not a dozen paces from the door.

I listened for the breathing of the sleeping woman. I worried that my appearance there would terrify her. If I could hear her breathe, I thought, I would go quietly away and find a hotel in which to sleep. I listened minute after minute, but I could not hear a sound.

At last I put my mouth to the keyhole and spoke to her. 'Jacqueline,' I called, and waited.

There was no answer. Then a little louder: 'Jacqueline! *Jacqueline!*'

Dead silence followed.

Then, out of the silence, I heard the loud ticking of the little alarm clock that I had left on the mantel of the bedroom. Perhaps if I waited a little longer, I should hear her breathing. But I could hear nothing. I took the key of the apartment door from my pocket at last and fitted it noiselessly into the lock. With shaking fingers, I turned the key.

The door creaked open. I caught at the door-edge, missed it and, tripping over a rent in the cheap mat that lay against the door inside, stumbled against the table edge and clung there.

The room was completely dark, except for a little patch of light high up on the bedroom wall, which came through a hole the workmen had made when they began demolishing the building. I hesitated a moment; then I drew a match from my pocket and lit it.

I reached up to the gas above the table, turned it on, and lit the incandescent mantle, lowering the light immediately.

But even then there was no sound from behind the curtains. They hung down close together, so that I was able to see only the gas-blackened ceiling above them and, underneath, the lower edge of the bed linen, and the bed-frame at the base, with its enameled iron feet. The sheets hung straight, as though the bed had not been occupied; but, though there was no sound, I knew Jacqueline was at the back of the curtains.

The oppressive stillness was not that of solitude. She must be awake; she must be listening in terror. I went toward the curtains.

'Jacqueline!' I whispered. 'It is Paul, your friend. Are you safe, Jacqueline?'

Now I saw, under the curtains, what looked like the body of a very small animal. It might have been a woolly dog, and it was lying perfectly still.

I pulled aside the curtains and stood between them, and the scene stamped itself upon my brain, as clear as a photographic print, forever.

The woolly beast was the fur cap of a dead man who lay across the floor of the little room. One foot was extended underneath the bed, and the head reached to the bottom of the wall on the other side of the room. He lay upon his back, his eyes open and staring, his hands clenched, and his features twisted into a sneering smile. His fur overcoat, unbuttoned, disclosed a warm knit waistcoat of a gaudy pattern, across which ran the heavy links of a gold chain. There was a tiny hole in his breast, over the heart, from which a little blood had flowed. The wound had pierced the heart, and death had evidently been instantaneous.

It was the man whom I had seen staring at us across Herald Square.

Beside the window Jacqueline crouched, and at her feet lay the husky, watching me silently. In her hand she held a tiny, dagger-like knife with a thin red-stained blade. Her grey eyes, black in the gaslight, stared into mine, and there was neither fear nor recognition in them. She was fully dressed, and the bed had not been occupied.

'Jacqueline!' I cried in terror. I took the weapon from her hand, then raised her hands to my lips and caressed them. She seemed quite unresponsive. I laid them against my cheek. I called her by her name imploringly; I spoke to her, but she only looked at me and made no answer. Still it was evident to me that she heard and understood, for she looked at me in a puzzled way, as if I were a complete stranger. She did not seem to resent my presence there, and she did not seem afraid of the dead man. She seemed, in a kindly, patient manner, to be trying to understand the meaning of the situation.

'Jacqueline,' I cried, 'you are not hurt? Thank God you are not hurt. What has happened?'

'I don't know,' she answered. 'I don't know where I am.'

I put my arms about her. 'Jacqueline, dear, will you not try to think? I am Paul — your friend Paul. Do you not remember me?'

'No, *monsieur*,' she sighed.

'But, then, how did you come here, Jacqueline?' I asked.

'I do not know, Paul.'

That encouraged me a little. Evidently she remembered what I had just said to her. 'Where is your home, Jacqueline?'

'I do not know,' she answered in an apathetic voice, devoid of interest.

There was something more to be said, though it was hard. 'Jacqueline, who — was — *that*?'

'Who?' she inquired, looking at me with the same patient, wistful gaze.

'That man, Jacqueline. That dead man.'

'What dead man, Paul?' She was staring straight at the body, and at that moment I realized that she not only did not remember, but did not even see it.

The shock which she had received, supervening upon the nervous state in which she had been when I encountered her, had produced one of those mental inhibitions in which the mind, to save the reason, obliterates temporarily not only all memory of the past, but also all present sights and sounds which may serve to recall it. She looked idly at the body of the dead man, and I was sure that she saw nothing but the worn woodwork of the floor.

I saw that it was useless to say anything more upon this subject. 'You are very tired, Jacqueline?' I asked.

'Yes, *monsieur*,' she answered, leaning back against my arm.

'And you would like to sleep?'

'Yes, *monsieur*.'

I raised her in my arms and laid her on the bed, telling her to close her eyes and sleep. She was asleep almost immediately after her head rested upon the pillow. She breathed as softly as an infant.

I watched her for a while until I heard a distant clock strike three. This recalled me to the dangers of our situation. I struck a match and lit the gas in the bedroom. But the yellow glare was so ghastly and intolerable that I turned it down.

And then I set about the task before me.

3

Covering the Tracks

I thought quickly. Once, I had been able to play an active part among the men who were my associates in that adventurous life that lay so far behind me. But eight years of clerkship had reduced me to the condition of one who waits on the command of others. Now my irresolution vanished, and I was my old self once more.

The first task was the disposal of the body in such a way that suspicion would not attach itself to me after I had vacated the rooms the next morning. There was a fire-escape running up to the floor of that room on the outside of the house, though there was no egress to it. It had been put up by the landlord to satisfy the requirements of some new law; but had never been meant for use, and it was constructed of the flimsiest and cheapest ironwork. I saw that it would be possible by standing on a chair to swing myself up to the hole in the wall and reach down to the iron stairs up which, I assumed, the dead man had crept after I had given him the hint of Jacqueline's abode by emerging from the front door.

I raised the dead man in my arms, looking apprehensively toward the bed. I was afraid Jacqueline would awaken, but she slept heavily, undisturbed by the creaking of the sagging floor beneath its double burden. I put the fur cap on the grotesque, nodding dead head, and, pushing a chair toward the wall with my foot, mounted it and managed with a great effort to squeeze through the hole, pulling up the body with me as I did so.

Then I felt with my foot for the little platform at the top of the iron stairs outside, found it, and dropped. Afterward I dragged the dreadful burden down from the hole. I had not known that I was especially strong before, but somehow I managed to accomplish my wretched task.

I carried the dead man all the way down the fire escape, clinging and straining against the rotting, rusting bars, which bent and cracked beneath my weight and seemed about to break and drag down the entire structure from the wall. I hardly paused at the platforms outside the successive stories. The weather was growing very cold, a storm was coming up, and the wind soughed and whined dismally around the eaves.

I reached the bottom at last and rested for a moment. At the back of the house was a little vacant space, filled with heaps of debris from the demolished portions of the building and with refuse which had been dumped there by tenants who had left and had never been removed. This yard was separated only by a rotting fence with a single wooden rail from a small blind alley.

The alley had run between rows of stables in former days when this was a fashionable quarter, but now these were mostly unoccupied, save for a few more pretentious ones at the lower end, which were being converted into garages. Everywhere were heaps of brick, piles of rain-rotted wood, and rubbish heaps.

I took up my burden and placed it at the end of the alley, covering it roughly with some old burlap bags which lay there. I thought it safe to assume that the police would look upon the dead man as the victim of some footpad. It was only remotely possible that suspicion would be directed against any occupant of any of the houses bordering on the cul-de-sac.

I did not search the dead man's pockets. I cared nothing who he was, and did not want to know. My sole desire was to acquit Jacqueline of his death in the world's eyes. That he had come deservedly by it I was positive. I was her sole protector now, and I felt a furious resolve that no one should rob me of her.

The ground was as hard as iron, and I was satisfied that my footsteps had left no track; there would be snow before morning, and if my feet had left any traces these would be covered effectively.

Four o'clock was striking while I was climbing back into the room again. Jacqueline lay on the bed in the same position; she had not stirred during that hour. While she slept, I set about the completion of my task. I took the knife from the floor where I had flung it, scrubbed it, and placed it in my suitcase. Then I scrubbed the floor clean, afterward rubbing it with a soiled rag to make its appearance uniform.

I washed my hands, and thought I had finally removed all traces of the affair; but, coming back, I perceived something upon the floor which had escaped my notice. It was the leather collar of the husky, with its big silver studs and the maker's silver nameplate. All this while the animal had remained perfectly quiet in the room crouching at Jacqueline's feet and beside the bed. It had not attempted to molest me, as I had feared might be the case during the course of my gruesome work.

I came to the conclusion that there might have been a struggle; that it had run to its mistress's assistance, and that the collar had been torn from it by the dead man. My first thought was to put the collar back upon the creature's neck; but then I came to the conclusion that this might possibly serve as a means of identification. And it was essential that no one should be able to identify the dog.

So I picked the collar up and carried it into the next room and held it under the light of the incandescent gas-mantle. The letters of the maker's name were almost obliterated, but after a careful study I was able to make them out. The name was Maclay & Robitaille, and the place of manufacture Quebec. This confirmed my belief concerning Jacqueline's nativity.

I pried the plate from the leather and slipped it into my pocket. I put the broken collar into my suitcase, together with the dagger, and then I set about packing my things for the journey which we were to undertake.

I had always accustomed myself to travel with a minimum of baggage, and the suitcase, which was a roomy one, held all that I should need at any time. When I had finished packing, I went back to Jacqueline and sat beside her while she slept. As I sat down, I heard a city clock strike five. In a little while it would begin to lighten, and the advent of the day filled me with a sort of terror.

I watched the sleeping woman. Who

was she? How could she sleep calmly after that night's deed? The mystery seemed unfathomable; the woman alone in the city, the robbers, the dog, the dead man, and the one who had escaped me.

Jacqueline's bag lay on the bureau, disgorging bills. There were rolls and rolls of them — eight thousand dollars did not seem too much. Besides these, the bag contained the usual feminine properties: a handkerchief, sachet-bag, a pocket mirror, and some thin papers coated with rice powder. The thought crossed my mind that the bills might be counterfeit, and I picked one up and looked carefully at it, comparing it with one from my own pocketbook. But I was soon satisfied that they were real.

Her soft brown hair streamed over the pillow and hung down toward the floor, a heavy mass, uncoiled from the wound braids upon her neck. Her breast rose and fell steadily with her breathing. She looked even younger than on the preceding evening. I was sure now that she was innocent of evil. Her outstretched arm was extended beyond the edge of the bed.

I raised her hand and held in it my own, and I sat thus until the room began to lighten, watching her all the while. It was strange that as I sat there I began to grow comforted. I looked on her as mine. When I had kissed her hands I had forgotten the ring upon her finger; and now, holding that hand in mine and running my fingers round and round the circlet of gold, I was not troubled at all. I could not think of her as any other man's. She was mine — Jacqueline.

Presently she stirred, her eyes opened, and she sat up. I placed a pillow at her back. She gazed at me with apathy, but there was also recognition in her look.

'Do you know me, Jacqueline?' I asked.

'Yes, Paul,' she answered.

'Your friend?'

'My friend, Paul.'

'Jacqueline, I am going to take you home,' I said, hoping that she would tell me something. I meant to take her to Quebec and make inquiries there. Thus I hoped to learn something of her, even if the sight of the town did not awaken her memories.

'Yes, Paul,' she answered in that docile manner of hers.

'It is lucky you have your furs, because the winter is cold where your home is.'

'Yes, Paul,' she repeated as before. Further probing on my part convinced me that she remembered nothing at all. Her mind was like a person's newly awakened in a strange land. But this state brought with it no fear, only a peaceful quietude and faith which was very touching.

'We have forgotten a lot of things that troubled us, haven't we, Paul?' she asked me presently. 'But we shall not care, since we have each other for friends. And afterwards perhaps we shall pick them up again. Do you not think so, Paul?'

'Yes, Jacqueline,' I answered.

'If we remembered now, the memory of them might make us unhappy,' she continued wistfully, a vague alarm in her eyes.

'Yes, Jacqueline,' I agreed. 'Now,' I continued, 'we need to make ready for our journey.'

I had just remembered that the storage company which was to warehouse my few belongings was to call that day. The van would probably be at the house early in the morning, and it was essential that we should be gone before it arrived. Fortunately I had arranged to leave the door unlocked in case my arrangements necessitated my early departure, and this was understood, so that my absence would cause no surprise.

I showed Jacqueline the bathroom and drew the curtains. Then I went into the kitchenette, brewed coffee on the gas range, and made some toast and buttered it. When I took in the breakfast, Jacqueline was waiting for me, looking very dainty and charming. She was hungry, too; also a good sign.

She did not seem to understand that there was anything strange in the situation in which we found ourselves. I did not know whether this was due to her mental state or to that strange unsophistication which I had already observed in her. At any rate, we ate our breakfast together as naturally as though we were an old married couple.

After the meal was ended, and we had fed the dog, Jacqueline insisted on washing the dishes, and I showed her the kitchenette and let her do so, though I should never have need for the cheap plates and cups again.

'Now, Jacqueline, we must go,' I said.

I placed her neckpiece about her. I closed her bag, stuffing the bills inside, and hung it on her arm. I could not resist a smile to see the little pad covered with its maze of figures among the rolls of money. I was afraid that the sight of it would awaken her memories, but she only looked quietly at it and put it away.

I wanted her to let me bank her money for her, but did not like to ask her. However, of her own account she took out the bills and handed them to me. 'What a lot of money I have,' she said. 'I hardly thought there was so much money in the world, Paul.'

It was past eight when we left the house. I carried my suitcase and, stopping at a neighbouring express office, had it sent to the Grand Central station. And then I decided to take the dog to the animal home.

I did not like to do so, but was afraid,

in the necessity of protecting Jacqueline, that its presence might possibly prove embarrassing, so I took it there and left it, with instructions that it was to be kept until I sent for it. I paid a small sum of money and we departed, Jacqueline apparently indifferent to what I had done, though the animal's distress at being parted from her disturbed my conscience a good deal. Still, it seemed the only thing to do under our circumstances.

Quebec, then, was my objective, and with no further clue than the dog collar. There were two trains, I found, at three and at nine. The first, which I proposed to take, would bring us to our destination soon after nine the next day; but our morning was to be a busy one, and it would be necessary to make our preparations quickly.

A little snow was on the ground, but the sun shone brightly, and I felt that the shadows of the night lay behind us.

4

Simon Leroux

With Jacqueline's arm drawn through mine, I paid a visit to the bank in which I had deposited my legacy, and drew out fifteen hundred dollars, next depositing Jacqueline's money to my own account. It amounted to almost exactly eight thousand dollars.

The receiving teller must have thought me an eccentric to carry so large a sum, and from his smile I know he thought that Jacqueline and I had just been married, for I saw him smile over the entry that he made in my bank book. I wanted to deposit her money in her own name, but this would have involved inquiries and explanations which I was not in a position to satisfy. So there was nothing to do but deposit it in my own, and afterward I could refund it to her.

We were exactly like a honeymoon couple. Although I endeavored to maintain an air of practical self-assurance, there was now a new shyness in her manner, an atmosphere of undefinable but very real sweetness in the relationship between us which set my heart hammering at times when I looked at her flushed cheeks and the fair hair, blown about her face, and hiding the glances which she stole timidly at me. It was like a honeymoon departure, only with another man's wife; and that set a seal of honour on me which must remain unbroken till the time arrived.

I wondered, as we strolled up Fifth Avenue together, how much she knew, what she remembered, and what thoughts went coursing through her head. That child-like faith of hers was an innocent confidence, but it was devoid of weakness. I believed that she was dimly aware that terrible things lay in the past and that she trusted to her forgetfulness as a shield to shelter not only herself but me, and would not voluntarily recall what she had forgotten.

It was necessary to buy her an outfit of clothes, and this problem worried me a good deal. I hardly knew the names of the things she required. I was afraid that she would not know what to buy; but, as the morning wore away, I realized that her mental faculties were not dimmed in the least. She observed everything, clapped her hands joyously as a child at the street sights and sounds, turned to wonder at the elevated and at the high buildings. I ventured, therefore, upon the subject of clothes.

'Jacqueline, you know that you will require an outfit of clothes before we start for your home. Not too many things — just enough for a journey.'

'Yes, Paul,' she answered.

'How much money will you need?'

'Fifty dollars?' she inquired.

I gave her a hundred, and we entered a large department store, and I mustered up enough courage to address the young woman who stood behind the counter that displayed an assortment of women's garments.

'I want a complete outfit for — for this lady,' I stammered. 'Enough for a two weeks' journey.'

The young woman smiled in a very pleasant way, and two others, who were near enough to have overheard, turned and smiled also.

'Bermuda or Niagara Falls?' asked the young woman.

'I beg your pardon?' I inquired, conscious that my face was insufferably hot.

'If you are taking *madame* to Bermuda, she will naturally require cooler clothing than if you are taking her to Niagara Falls,' the young woman explained, looking at me with benevolent patience. 'Perhaps *madame* might prefer to make her own selection.'

As I stood in the centre of the store, Jacqueline flitted here and there, until a comfortable assortment of parcels was accumulated upon the counter.

'Where shall I send them, *madame*?' inquired the saleswoman.

There was a suitcase to be bought, so I had them transferred to the trunk and leather-goods department, where I bought a neat sole-leather suitcase which, at Jacqueline's practical suggestion, was changed for a lighter one of plaited straw.

Everybody addressed her as *madame*, and everybody smiled on us, and sometimes I reflected miserably upon the wedding ring.

I had considered taking her into

Tiffany's to buy her a trinket of some kind, when something happened which put the idea completely out of my head. While Jacqueline was examining the suitcases, my attention was drawn to a tall elderly man with a hard, drawn, and deeply lined weather-beaten face, and wearing a massive fur overcoat, open in front, who was standing in the division between the trunk department and that adjoining it, immediately behind Jacqueline. He was looking at me with an unmistakable glance of recognition.

I knew that I had seen him several times before, but, though his features were familiar, I had forgotten his name. I stared at him and he stared back at me, and made an urgent sign to me.

Keeping an eye on Jacqueline, I followed the tall man. As I neared him, my remembrance of him grew stronger. I knew that powerful, slouching gait, that heavy tread. When he turned round, I had his name on my lips.

It was Simon Leroux.

'So you've got her!' he began in a hoarse, forcible whisper. 'Where did you pick her up? I was hurrying away from Tom's office when I happened to see you two entering Mischenbusch's.'

I remembered then that the office in which I had drudged was only a couple of blocks away. I made no answer, but waited for him to lead again — and I was thinking hard.

'There's the devil to pay!' he went on in his accent. 'Louis came on posthaste, as you know, and he hasn't turned up this morning yet. Ah, I always knew Tom was close, but I never dreamed *you* knew anything. When I used to see you sitting near the door in his office writing in those *sacré* books, I thought you were just a clerk. And you were in the know all the time, you were! You know what happened last night?' he continued, looking furtively around.

'It was an unfortunate affair,' I said guardedly.

'Unfortunate! It was the devil, by gosh! Who was he?'

His face was fiery red, and he cast so keen a look at me that I almost thought he had discovered he was betraying himself.

'It was lucky I was in New York when Louis wired us she had flown,' he continued, swearing an oath. 'Lucky I had my men with me, too. I didn't think I'd need them here, but I'd promised them a trip to New York — and then comes Louis's wire. I put them on the track. I guessed she'd go to Daly's — old Duchaine was mad about that crazy system of his, and had been writing to him.

'He used to know Daly when they were young men together at Saratoga and Montreal, and in Quebec, in the times when they had good horses and high play there. I tell you it was ticklish. There was millions of dollars' worth of property walking up Broadway, and they'd got her, with a taxi waiting nearby, when that devil's fool strolls up and draws a crowd. If I'd been there, I'd have — '

A string of vile expletives followed his last remark.

'They got on his track and followed them to the Merrimac,' he continued. 'And they never came out. They waited all night till nine this morning, and they never came out. My God, I thought her a good woman — it's awful! Who was he? Say, how much do you know?'

His face was dripping with sweat, and he shot an awful look at Jacqueline as she bent over the suitcase. I remembered now that, after sending Jacqueline to the clerk's desk alone, she had gone to a side entrance and I had joined her there and left the hotel with her in that fashion. At any rate, Simon's words showed me that his hired men were not acquainted with the rest of the night's work.

I gathered from what he had said that the possession of Jacqueline was vitally important both to Leroux and to Tom Carson, for some reason connected with the Northern Exploitation Company, and that they had tried to kidnap her and hold her till the man Louis arrived to advise them.

'How much do you know?' hissed Simon.

'Leroux,' I said, 'I'm not going to tell you anything. You will remember that I was employed by Mr. Carson.'

'Ain't I as good as Carson? What are

you going to do with her?'

'You'd better go back to the office and wait, unless you want to spoil the game by letting her see you,' I said.

I was sure he was hiding from her intentionally, and I could see that he believed I was working for Carson, for though he scowled fearfully at me, he seemed impressed by my words.

'I don't know whether Tom's running straight or not,' he said huskily; 'but let me tell you, young man, it'll pay you to keep in with me, and if you've got any price, name it!'

He shook his heavy fist over me — I believe the clerks thought he was going to strike me, for they came hurrying toward us. But I saw Jacqueline approaching, and, without another word, Leroux turned away.

Jacqueline caught sight of his retreating figure and her eyes widened. I thought I saw a shadow of fear in them. Then the memory was effaced and she was smiling again.

I instructed the store to call a messenger and have the suitcase taken at once to the baggage room in the Grand Central station.

'Now, Jacqueline, I'm going to take you to lunch,' I said. 'And afterward we will start for home.'

Outside the store, I looked carefully around and espied Leroux almost immediately lighting a cigar in the doorway of a shop. I hit upon a rather daring plan to escape him. Carson's offices were in a large modern building, with many elevators and entrances. I walked toward it with Jacqueline, being satisfied that Leroux was following us; entered about twenty-five yards before him, and ascended in the elevator, getting off, however, on the floor above that on which the offices were.

I was satisfied that Leroux would follow me a minute later, under the impression that we had gone to the Northern Exploitation Company; and so, after waiting a minute or two, I took Jacqueline down in another elevator, and we escaped through the front entrance and jumped into a taxi-cab.

I was satisfied that I had thrown Leroux off the scent, but I took the precaution to stop at a gunsmith's shop and purchase a pair of automatic pistols and a hundred cartridges. The man would not sell them to me there on account of the law, but he promised to put them in a box and have them delivered at the station, and there, in due course, I found them.

But I was very uneasy until we found ourselves in the train. And then at last everything was accomplished — our baggage upon the seats beside us and our berths secured. At three precisely the train pulled out, and Jacqueline nestled down beside me, and we looked at each other and were happy.

And then, at the very moment when the wheels began to revolve, Leroux stepped down from a neighbouring train. As he passed our window, he espied us. He started and glared, and then he came racing back toward us, shaking his fists and yelling vile expletives. He tried to swing himself aboard in his fury despite the fact that the doors were all shut. A porter pushed him back, and the last I saw of him he was still pursuing us, screaming with rage.

I knew that he would follow on the nine o'clock train, reaching Quebec about five the following afternoon. That gave us five hours' grace. It was not much, but it was something to have Jacqueline safe with me even until the morrow.

I turned toward her, fearful that she had recognized the man and realized the situation. But she was smiling happily at my side, and I was confident then that, by virtue of that same mental inhibition, she had neither seen nor heard the fellow.

She looked at me thoughtfully a minute. 'Paul, when we get home — '

'Jacqueline?'

'I do not know,' she said, putting her palms to her head. 'Perhaps I shall remember then. But you — you must stay with me, Paul.'

Her lips quivered slightly. She turned her head away and looked out of the window at the horrible maze of houses in the Bronx and the disfiguring signboards.

New York was slipping away. All my old life was slipping away like this — and evil following us. I slipped one of the automatics out of my suitcase into my pocket and swore that I would guard Jacqueline from any shadow of harm.

One question recurred to my mind incessantly. Could she be ignorant that she had a husband somewhere? Would she tell me — or was this the chief of the memories that she had laid aside?

I opened one of the newspapers that I had bought at the station bookstand, dreading to find in flaring letters the headlines announcing the discovery of the body. I found the announcement — but in small type. The murder was ascribed to a gang battle — the man could not be identified, and apparently both police and public considered the affair merely one of those daily slayings that occur in that city.

Another newspaper devoted about the same amount of space to the account, but it published a photograph of the dead man, taken in the alley, where, it appeared, the reporter had viewed the body before it had been removed. The photograph looked horribly lifelike. I cut it out and placed it in my pocketbook.

For the present I felt safe. I believed the

affair would be forgotten soon. And meanwhile here was Jacqueline. She was asleep at my side, and her head drooped on my shoulder. We sat thus all the afternoon, while the city disappeared behind us, and we passed through Connecticut and approached the Vermont hills.

Then we had a light supper in the dining car. Afterward I walked to the car entrance and flung the broken dog collar away across the fields. That was the last link that bound us to the past.

Then the berths were lowered and made up; and fastening from my upper place the curtain which fell before Jacqueline's, I knew that, for one night more, at least, I held her in safe ward.

5

M. Le Curé

The very obvious decision at which I arrived after a night of cogitation in my berth was that Jacqueline was to pass as my sister. I explained my plan to her at breakfast.

There had been the examination of baggage at the frontier and the tiresome change to a rear car in the early morning, and most of us were heavy-eyed, but she looked as fresh and charming as ever in her new waist of black lace and the serge skirt which she had bought the day before. It seemed impossible to realize that I was really seated opposite her in the dining car, talking amid the chatter of a party of red-cheeked French-Canadian schoolchildren who had come on the train at Sherbrooke, homeward bound for the approaching Christmas holidays.

'You see, Jacqueline,' I explained, 'it

will look strange our travelling together, unless some close relationship is supposed to exist between us. So I shall call you my sister, Miss Hewlett, and you will call me your brother Paul.' And I handed her my visiting card, because she had never heard my surname before.

'I shall be glad to think of you as my brother Paul,' she answered, looking at the card. She held it in her right hand, and it was not until the middle of the meal that the left hand came into view. Then I discovered that she had taken off her wedding ring. I wondered what thought impelled her to do this.

We sped northward all that morning, stopping at many little wayside stations, and as we rushed along beside the ice-bound St. Francis the air ever grew colder, and the land, deep in snow, and the tall pines, white with frost, looked like a picture on a Christmas card. At last the St. Lawrence appeared, covered with drifting floes; the Isle of Orleans, with the Falls of Montmorency behind it; the ascending heights which slope up to the *Chateau* Frontenac, the fort-crowned citadel, the long parapet, bristling with guns.

Then, after the ferry had transferred us from Levis, we stood in Lower Quebec. We had hardly gone on board the ferryboat when an incident occurred that greatly disturbed me. A slightly built well-dressed man with a small upturned mustache and a face of notable pallor passed and repassed us several times, staring and smiling with cool effrontery at both of us. He wore a lambskin cap and a fur overcoat, and I could not help associating him with the dead man, or avoiding the belief that he had travelled north with us, and that Leroux had been to see him off at the station.

I was a good deal troubled by this, but before I had decided to address the fellow, we landed, and a sleigh swept us up the hill toward the *château* to the tune of jingling bells. It was a strange wintry scene — the low sleighs, their drivers wrapped in furs and capped in bearskin, the hooded nuns in the streets, the priests, soldiers, and ancient houses. The air was keen and dry.

'This is Quebec, Jacqueline,' I said.

I thought that she remembered unwillingly, but she said nothing. I fancied that each scene brought back its own memories, but not the ideas associated with the chain of scenes.

We secured adjacent rooms at the *château*, and leaving Jacqueline to unpack her things, and under instructions not to leave her room and promising to return as soon as possible, I started out at once to find Maclay & Robitaille's.

This proved a task of no great difficulty. It was a little shop where leather goods were sold, situated on St. Joseph Street. A young man with a dark clean-shaven face was behind the counter. He came forward courteously as I approached.

'I have come on an unusual mission,' I began foolishly, then stopped. I must have aroused his suspicions immediately.

He begged my pardon and called a man from another part of the shop. And that gave me my chance over again, for I realized that he had not understood my English.

'Do you remember,' I asked the newcomer, 'selling a collar to a young lady recently — a dog collar, I mean?'

The proprietor shrugged. 'I sell a good many dog collars during the year.'

I took the plate from my pocket and set it down on the counter. 'The collar was set with silver studs,' I said. 'This was the plate.' Then I remembered the name Leroux had used and flung it out at random. 'I think it was for a Mlle. Duchaine,' I added.

The shot went home.

'Ah, *monsieur*, now I remember perfectly,' answered the proprietor, 'both from the unusual nature of the collar and from the fact that there was some difficulty in delivering it. There was no post office nearer the seigniory than St. Boniface, where it lay unclaimed for a long time. I think *mademoiselle* had forgotten all about the order. Or perhaps the dog had died!'

'Where is this *seigniory*?'

'The *seigniory* of M. Charles Duchaine?' he answered, looking curiously at me. 'You are evidently a stranger, *monsieur*, or you would have heard of it, especially now when people are saying that — ' He checked himself at this point. 'It is the oldest of the *seigniories*,' he continued. 'In fact, it has never passed out of the hands of the original owners, because it is almost uninhabitable in winter, except by Indians. I understand that M. Duchaine has built himself a fine *château* there; but then he is a recluse *monsieur*, and probably not ten men have ever visited it. But *mademoiselle* is too fine a woman to be imprisoned there long — '

'How could one reach the *château*?' I interpolated.

He looked at me inquiringly as though he wondered what my business there could be. 'In summer,' he replied, 'one might ascend the Rivière d'Or in a canoe for half the distance, until one reached the mountains, and then — ' He shrugged his shoulders. 'I do not know. Possibly one would inquire of the first trapper who passed in autumn. In winter one would fly. It is strange that so little is known of the *seigniory*, for they say the Rivière d'Or — '

'The Golden River?'

'Has vast wealth in it, and formerly the Indians would bring gold dust in quills to the traders. But many have sought the source of this supply in past times and failed or died, and so — ' He shrugged again. 'You see, M. Duchaine is a hermit,' he continued. 'Once, so my father used to say, he was one of the gayest young men in Quebec. But he became involved in the troubles of 1867 — and then his wife died, and so he withdrew there with the little *mademoiselle* — what was her name?' He called his clerk. 'Alphonse, what is the name of that pretty daughter of M. Charles Duchaine, of Rivière d'Or?' he asked.

'Annette,' answered the man. 'No, Janette. I am sure it ends with 'ette' or 'ine,' anyway.'

'*Eh bien*, it makes no difference,' said the proprietor, 'because, since she left the Convent of the Ursulines here in Quebec, where she was educated, her father keeps her at the *château*, and you are not likely to set eyes on M. Charles Duchaine's daughter.'

A sudden stoppage in his flow of words, an almost guilty look upon his face, as a new figure entered the little shop, directed my attention toward the stranger. He was an old man of medium size, very muscularly built, stout, and with enormous shoulders. He wore a priest's soutane, but he did not look like a priest — he looked like a man's head on a bull's body. His smooth face was tanned to the colour of an Indian's — his bright blue eyes, almost concealed by their drooping, wrinkled lids, were piercing in their scrutiny.

He wore a bearskin hat and furs of surprising quality. It was not so much his strange appearance that attracted my interest as the singular look of authority upon the face, which was yet deeply lined about the mouth, as though he could relax upon occasion and become the jolliest of companions. And he spoke a pure French, interspersed with words of an uncouth *patois*, which I ascribed to long residence in some remote parish.

'*Bo'jour*, Père Antoine,' said the shop-keeper deferentially, fixing his eyes rather timidly upon the old priest's face.

'*Eh bien*, who is this with whom thou gossip concerning the daughter of M. Duchaine?' inquired Father Antoine, looking at me keenly.

'Only a customer — a stranger, *monsieur*,' answered the proprietor. 'He wishes to see — a dog collar, was it not?' he continued, turning nervously toward me.

'You talk too much,' said Père Antoine roughly. 'Now, *monsieur*,' he said, addressing me in fair English, 'what is the nature of your business that it can possibly concern either M. Duchaine or his daughter? Perhaps I can inform you, since he is one of my parishioners.'

'My conversation was not with you, *monsieur le curé*,' I answered shortly, and left the shop. I had ascertained what I needed to know, and had no desire to enter into a discussion of my business with the old man.

I had not gone three paces from the door, however, when the priest, coming up behind me, placed a huge hand upon my shoulder and swung me around without the least apparent effort.

'I do not know what your business is, *monsieur*,' he said, 'but if it were an honest one you would state it to me. If you wish to see M. Duchaine, I am best qualified to assist you to do so, since I visit his *château* twice each year to carry the consolations of religion to him and his people. But if your business is not honest it will fail. End it then and return to your own country.'

'I do not intend to discuss my business with you, *monsieur*,' I answered angrily.

He let me go and stood eyeing me with his keen gaze. I jumped on a passing car, but looking back, I saw him striding along behind it. He seemed to walk as quickly as the car went through the crowded street, and with no effort.

When I got off in the neighbourhood of the Place d'Armes, it was nearly dark; but though I could not see the old man, I was convinced that he was still following me.

I found Jacqueline in her room looking over her purchases, and took her down to dinner. And here I had another disconcerting experience, for hardly were we seated when the inquisitive stranger whom I had seen at the ferry came into the dining room, and after a careful survey which ended as his eyes fell on us, he took his seat at an adjacent table. I could not but connect him with our presence there.

Leroux was due to arrive at any moment. I realized that great issues were at stake, and that the man would never cease in his attempts to get hold of Jacqueline. Only when I had returned her to her father's house would I feel safe from him.

The *château* was the worst place to have made my headquarters. If I had realized the man's persistence, perhaps I would have sought less conspicuous lodgings. Leroux's behaviour at the railroad station had betrayed both an ungovernable temper when he was crossed, and to a certain extent, fearlessness. Nevertheless, I believed him to have also an elemental cunning which would dissuade him from violent measures so long as we were in Quebec. I resolved, therefore, not to avoid him, but to await his lead.

After dinner I had some conversation

with one of the hotel clerks. I discovered that the Rivière d'Or flowed into the Gulf of St. Lawrence from the north, in the neighbourhood of Anticosti. It was a small stream, and except for a postal station at its mouth named St. Boniface, was little known, the only occupants of those parts being trappers and Indians.

When I told the clerk that I had business at St. Boniface, I think he concluded that I represented an amalgamation of fishing interests, for he became exceedingly communicative. 'You could hire dogs and a sleigh at St. Boniface for wherever your final destination is,' he said, 'because the dog mail has been suspended owing to the new government mail boats, and the sleighs are idle. I think Captain Dubois would take you on his boat as far as that point, and I believe he makes his next trip in a couple of days.'

He gave me the captain's address, and I resolved to call on him early the following day and make arrangements. I was just turning away when I saw the inquisitive stranger leave the smoking room. He crossed the hall and went out, not without bestowing a long look on me.

'Who is that man?' I asked.

'Why, isn't he a friend of yours?' inquired the clerk.

'Only by the way he stares at me,' I said.

'Well, he said he thought he knew you and asked me your name,' the clerk answered. 'He didn't give me his, and I don't think he has been in here before.'

I took Jacqueline for a stroll on the Terrace, and while we walked I pondered over the problem.

The night was too beautiful for my depression of mind to last. The stars blazed brilliantly overhead; upon our left the faint outlines of the Laurentians rose, in front of us the lights of Levis twinkled above the frozen gulf. There was a flicker of northern lights in the sky. We paced the Terrace, arm in arm, from the statue of Champlain that overlooks the Place d'Armes to the base of the mighty citadel, and back, till the cold drove us in.

Jacqueline was very quiet, and I wondered what she remembered. I dreaded always awakening her memory lest, with that of her home, came that other of the dead man.

Our rooms were on the side of the *château* facing the town, and as we passed beneath the arch I saw two men standing no great distance away, and watching us, it seemed to me. One wore the cassock of a priest, and I could have sworn that he was Père Antoine; the other resembled the inquisitive stranger. As we drew near, they moved behind a pillar. Thus, inexorably, the chase drew near.

My suspicions received confirmation a few minutes later, for we had hardly reached our rooms, and I was, in fact, standing at the door of Jacqueline's, bidding her good night, when a bellboy came along the passage and announced that the gentleman whom I was expecting was coming up the stairs.

I said good night to Jacqueline and went into my room and waited. I had thought it would be the stranger, but it was the priest. I invited him to enter, and he came in and stood with his fur cap on his head, looking direfully at me.

'Well, *monsieur*, what is the purpose of this visit?' I asked.

'To tell you,' he thundered, 'that you must give up the unhappy woman who has accompanied you here.'

'That is precisely what I intend to do,' I answered.

'To me,' he said. 'Her husband.'

I felt my brain whirling. I knew now that I had always cherished a hope, despite the ring — what a fool I had been!

'I married them,' continued Père Antoine.

'Where is he?' I demanded desperately. He appeared disconcerted. I gathered from his stare that he had supposed I knew.

'This is a Catholic country,' he went on more quietly. 'There is no divorce; there can be none. Marriage is a sacrament. Sinning as she is — '

I placed my hand on his shoulder. 'I will not hear any more,' I said. 'Go!' I pointed toward the door.

'I am going to take her away with me,' he said, and crossing the threshold into the corridor, placed one hand on the door of Jacqueline's room.

I got there first. I thrust him violently aside — it was like pushing a monument; then turned the key, which happily was still outside, and put it in my pocket.

'I am ready to deal with her husband,' I said. 'I am not ready to deal with you. Leave at once, or I will have you arrested, priest or no priest.'

He raised his arm threateningly. 'In God's name — ' he began.

'In God's name you shall not interfere with me,' I cried. 'Tell that to your confederate, Simon Leroux. A pretty priest you are!' I raged. 'How do I know she has a husband? How do I know you are not in league with her persecutors? How do I know you are a priest at all?'

He seemed amazed at the violence of my manner. 'This is the first time my priesthood has been denied,' he said quietly. 'Well, I have offered you your chance. I cannot use violence. If you refuse, you will bring your own punishment upon your head, and hers on that of the unhappy woman whom you have led into sin.'

'Go!' I shouted, pointing down the passage.

He turned and went, his soutane sweeping against the door of Jacqueline's room as he went by. At the entrance to the elevator he turned again and looked back steadily at me. Then the door clanged and the elevator went down.

I unlocked the door of Jacqueline's room. I saw her standing at the foot of the bed. She was supporting herself by her hands on the brass framework. Her face was white. As I entered, she looked up piteously at me.

'Who — was — that?' she asked in a frightened whisper.

'An impudent fellow — that is all, Jacqueline.'

'I thought I knew his voice,' she answered slowly. 'It made me — almost — remember. And I do not *want* to remember, Paul.'

She put her arms about my neck and cried. I tried to comfort her, but it was a long time before I succeeded.

I locked her door on the outside, and that night I slept with the key beneath by pillow.

6

At the Foot of the Cliff

The next morning, after again cautioning Jacqueline not to leave her room until I returned, I went to the house of Captain Dubois on Paul Street, in the Lower Town.

I was admitted by a pleasant-looking woman who told me that the captain would not be home until three in the afternoon, so I returned to the *château*, took Jacqueline for a sleigh ride round the fortifications, and delighted her, and myself also, by the purchase of two fur coats, heavy enough to exclude the biting cold which I anticipated we should experience during our journey.

In the afternoon I went back to Paul Street and found M. Dubois at home. He was a man of agreeable appearance, a typical Frenchman of about forty-five, with a full face sparsely covered with a black beard that was beginning to turn grey at the sides, and with an air of sagacious understanding in which I detected both sympathy and a lurking humour.

When I explained that I wanted to secure two passages to St. Boniface, his brows contracted. 'So you, too, are going to the *Château* Duchaine!' he exclaimed. 'Is there not room for two more on the boat of Captain Duhamel?'

I disclaimed all knowledge of Duhamel, but he looked entirely unconvinced.

'It is a pity, *monsieur*, that you are not acquainted with Captain Duhamel,' he said dryly, 'because I cannot take you to St. Boniface. But undoubtedly Captain Duhamel will assist you and your friend on your way to the *Château* Duchaine.'

'Why do you suppose that I am going to the *Château* Duchaine?' I inquired angrily.

He flared up, too. '*Diable!*' he burst out. 'Do you suppose all Quebec does not know what is in the wind? But since you are so ignorant, *monsieur*, I will enlighten you. We will assume, to begin then, that you are not going to the *château*, but only to St. Boniface, perhaps to engage in fishing for your support, eh, *monsieur?*'

Here he looked mockingly at my fur coat, which hardly bore out this presumption of my indigence.

'*Eh bien*, to continue. Let us suppose that the affairs of M. Charles Duchaine have interested a gentleman of business and politics whom we will call M. Leroux — just for the sake of giving him a name, you understand,' he resumed, looking at me maliciously. 'And that this M. Leroux imagines that there is more than spruce timber to be found on the seigniory. *Bien*, but consider further that this M. Leroux is a mole, as we call our politicians here. It would not suit him to appear openly in such an enterprise? He would always work through his agents in everything would he not, being a mole?

'Let us say then that he arranges with a Captain Duhamel to convey his party to St. Boniface, to which point he will go secretly by another route, and that he will join them there, and — in short, *monsieur*, take yourself and your friend to the devil, for I won't give you passage.'

His face was purple, and I assumed that he bore no love for Simon, whose name seemed to be of considerable importance in Quebec. I was delighted at the turn affairs were taking.

'You have not a very kindly feeling for this mythical person whom we have agreed to call Leroux,' I said.

Captain Dubois jumped out of his chair and raised his arms passionately above him. 'No, nor for any of his friends,' he answered. 'Go back to him — for I know he sent you to me — and tell him he cannot hire Alfred Dubois for all the money in Canada.'

'I am glad to hear you say that,' I answered, 'because Leroux is no friend of mine. Now listen to me, Captain Dubois. It is true that I am going to the *château*, if I can get there, but I did not know that Leroux had made his arrangements already. In brief, he is in pursuit of me, and I have urgent reasons for avoiding him. My companion is a lady — '

'Eh?' he exclaimed, looking stupidly at me.

'And I am anxious to take her to the *château*, where we shall be safe from the man — '

'A lady!' exclaimed the captain. 'A young one? Why didn't you tell me so at first, *monsieur!* I'll take you. I will do anything for an enemy of Leroux. He put my brother in jail on a false charge because he wouldn't bow to him — my brother died there, *monsieur* — that was his wife who opened the door to you. And the children, who might have starved, if I had not been able to take care of them! And he has tried to rob me of my position, only it is a Dominion one — the rascal!' The captain was becoming incoherent. He drew his sleeve across his eyes. 'But a lady!' he continued, with forced gaiety a moment later. 'I do not know your business, *monsieur*, but I can guess, perhaps — '

'But you must not misunderstand me,' I interposed. 'She is not — '

'It's all right!' said the captain, slapping me upon the back. 'No explanations! Not a word, I assure you. I am the most discreet of men. Madeleine!' This last word was a deep-chested bellow, and in response a little woman came running in, staggering under the weight of the captain's overcoat of raccoon fur. 'That is my overcoat voice,' he explained, stroking the child's head. 'My niece, *monsieur*. The others are boys. I wish they were all women, but God knows best. And, you see, a man can save much trouble, for by the tone in which I call, Madeleine knows whether it is my overcoat or my pipe or slippers that I want, or whether I am growing hungry.'

I thought that the captain's hunger voice must shake the rafters of the old building.

'And now, *monsieur*,' he continued seriously, when we had left the house, 'I am going to take you down to the pier and show you my boat. And I will tell you as much as I know concerning the plans of that scoundrel. In brief, it is known that a party of his friends has been quartered for some time at the *château*; they come and go, in fact, and now he is either taking more, or the same ones back again, and God knows why he takes them to so desolate a region, unless, as the rumour is, he has discovered coal fields upon the seigniory and holds M. Duchaine in his power. Well, *monsieur*, a party sails with Captain Duhamel on tonight's tide, which will carry me down the gulf also.

'You see, *monsieur*,' he continued, 'it is impossible to clear the ice unless the tide bears us down; but once the Isle of Orleans is past, we shall be in more open water and independent of the current. Captain Duhamel's boat is berthed at the same pier as mine upon the opposite side, for they both belong to the Saint Laurent Company, which leases them in winter.

'We start together, then, but I shall expect to gain several hours during the four days' journey, for I know the *Claire* well, and she cannot keep pace with my *Sainte-Vierge*. In fact it was only yesterday that the government arranged for me to take over the *Sainte-Vierge* in place of the *Claire*, which I have commanded all the winter, for it is essential that the mails reach St. Boniface and the maritime villages as quickly as possible. So you must bring your lady aboard the *Sainte-Vierge* by nine tonight.

'I shall telegraph to my friend Danton at St. Boniface to have a sleigh and dogs at your disposal when you arrive, and a tent, food, and sleeping bags,' continued Captain Dubois, 'for it must be a hundred and fifty miles from St. Boniface to the *Château* Duchaine. It is not a journey that a woman should take in winter,' he added with a sympathetic glance at me, 'but doubtless your lady knows the way and the journey well.'

The question seemed extraordinarily sagacious; it threw me into confusion.

'You see, M. Danton carried the mails by dog sleigh before the steamship winter mail service was inaugurated,' he went on, 'and now he will be glad of an opportunity to rent his animals. So I shall wire him tonight to hold them for you alone, and shall describe you to him. And thus we will check M. Leroux's designs, which have doubtless included this point. And so, with half a day's start, you will have nothing to fear from him — only remember that he has no scruples. Still, I do not think he will catch you and Mlle.

Jacqueline before you reach *Château* Duchaine,' he ended, chuckling at his sagacity.

'Ah, well, *monsieur*, who else could your lady be?' he asked, smiling at my surprise. 'I knew well that someday she must leave those wilds. Besides, did I not convey her here from St. Boniface on my return, less than a week ago, when she pleaded for secrecy? I suspected something agitated her then. So it was to find a husband that she departed thus? When she is home again, kneeling at her old father's feet, pleading for forgiveness, he will forgive — have no fear, *mon ami.*'

So Jacqueline had left her home not more than a week before! And the captain had no suspicion that she was married then! Yet Père Antoine claimed to have performed the ceremony. To whom? And where was the man who should have stood in my place and shielded her against Leroux?

I made Dubois understand, not without difficulty, that we were still unmarried. His face fell when he realized that I was in earnest, but after a little he made the best of the situation, though it was evident that some of the glamour was scratched from the romance in his opinion.

By now we had arrived at the wharf. It was a short pier at the foot of one of the numerous narrow streets that run down from the base of the mighty cliff which ascends to the ramparts and Park Frontenac. On either side, wedged in among the floes, lay a small ship of not many tons' burden — the *Claire* and the *Sainte-Vierge* respectively. The latter vessel lay upon our right as we approached the end of the wharf.

'Hallo! Hallo, Pierre!' shouted Dubois in what must have resembled his dinner voice, and a seaman with a short black beard came running up the deck and stopped at the gangway.

'It is all right,' said Dubois after a few moments' conversation. 'Pierre understands all that is necessary, and he will tell the men. And now I will show you the ship.'

There was a small cabin for Jacqueline and another for myself adjoining. This accommodation had been built for the convenience of the passengers whom the Saint-Laurent Company, though its boats were built for freight, occasionally accepted during its summer runs. I was very well satisfied and inquired the terms.

'If it were not for the children, there should be no terms!' exclaimed the captain. 'But it is hard, *monsieur*, with prices rising and the hungry mouths always open, like little birds.'

He was overjoyed at the sight of the fifty dollars which I tendered him. However, my generosity was not wholly disingenuous. I felt that it would be wise to make one staunch friend in that unfriendly city; and money does bind, though friendship exist already.

'By the way,' I said, 'do you know a priest named Père Antoine?'

'An old man? A strong old man? Why, assuredly, *monsieur*,' answered the captain. 'Everybody knows him. He has the parish of the Rivière d'Or district, and the largest in Quebec. As far as Labrador it is said to extend, and he covers it all twice each year, in his canoe or upon snowshoes. A saint, *monsieur*, as not all of our priests are, alas! You will do well to make his acquaintance.'

He placed one brawny hand upon my shoulder and swung me around. 'Now at last I understand!' he bellowed. 'So it is Père Antoine who is to make you and *mademoiselle* husband and wife! And you thought to conceal it from me, *monsieur*!' he continued reproachfully.

His good humour being completely restored by this prospective consummation of the romance, the captain parted from me on the wharf on his way to the telegraph office, repeating his instructions to the effect that we were to be aboard the boat by nine, as he would not be able to remain later than that hour on account of the tide.

It had grown dark long before and, looking at my watch, I was surprised to see that it was already past six o'clock. I had no time to lose in returning to the *château*. But though I could see it outlined upon the cliff, I soon found myself lost among the maze of narrow streets in which I was wandering. I asked the direction of one or two wayfarers, but these were all men of the labouring class, and their instructions, given in the provincial patois, were quite unintelligible to me.

A man was coming up the street behind me, and I turned to question him, but as I decreased my pace, he diminished his also, and when I quickened mine, he went faster as well. I began to have an uneasy sense that he might be following me, and accordingly hastened onward until I came to a road which seemed to lead up the hill toward the ramparts.

The *château* now stood some distance upon my left, but once I had reached the summit of the cliff it would only be a short walk away. The road, however, led me into a blind alley, the farther extremity being the base of the cliff; but another street emerged from it at a right angle, and I plunged into this, believing that any of the byways would eventually take me to the top of the acclivity.

As I entered this street, I heard the footsteps behind me quicken and, looking around, perceived that the man was close upon me. He stopped at the moment I did and disappeared in a small court. There was nothing remarkable in this, only to my straining eyes he seemed to bear a resemblance to the man with the patch whom I had encountered at the corner of Sixth Avenue on that night when I met Jacqueline.

I knew from Leroux's statement to me that the man had been a member of his gang. I was quite able to take care of myself under normal circumstances. But now — I was afraid. The mighty cliff before me, the silence of the deserted alleys in which I wandered helplessly, the thought of Jacqueline alone, waiting anxiously for my return, almost unmanned me. I felt like a hunted man, and my safety, upon which her own depended, attained an exaggerated importance in my mind.

So I almost ran forward into the byway which seemed to lead toward the summit, and as I did so I heard the footsteps close behind me again. I had entered one of the narrowest streets I had ever seen, and the most curious. It was just wide enough to admit the passage of a sleigh perhaps; the crumbling and dilapidated old houses, which seemed deserted, were connected overhead by a succession of wooden bridges, and those on my left were built into the solid rock, which rose sheer overhead.

In front of me the alley seemed to widen. I almost ran; but when I reached it I found that it was merely a bend in the passage, and the alley ran on straight as before. On my left hand was a tiny unfenced courtyard, not more than six yards in area, and I turned into this quickly and waited. I was confident that the bend in the street had hidden me from my pursuer; and, as I anticipated, he came on at a swifter rate. He was abreast of me when I put out my hand and grasped him by the coat, while with the other I felt in my pocket for my automatic pistol.

It was not there. I had left it in the pocket of the overcoat which I had changed at the furrier's shop and had sent to the *château*. And I was looking into the villainous face of the ruffian who had knocked me down on Sixth Avenue.

'What are you following me for?' I cried furiously.

He wrenched himself out of my grasp and pulled a long knife from his pocket. I caught him by the wrist, and we wrestled to and fro upon the snow. He pummeled me about the face with his free hand, but though I was no match for him in strength, he could not get the knife from me. The keen steel slashed my fingers, but the thought of Jacqueline helped me.

I got his hand open, snatched the knife, and flung it far away among the stunted shrubs that clung to the cliff-side. And we stood watching each other, panting.

He did not try to attack me again, but stood just out of my reach, grinning diabolically at me. His gaze shifted over my shoulder. Instinctively I swung around as the dry snow crackled behind me.

I was a second too late, for I saw nothing but the looming figure of a second ruffian and his upraised arm; then painless darkness seemed to enfold me, and I was conscious of plunging down into a fathomless abyss.

7

Captain Dubois

Clang! Clang! It sounded as though some titanic blacksmith were pounding on a mighty anvil to a devil's chorus of laughter. And I was bound to the steel, and each blow awakened hideous echoes which went resounding through my brain forever. *Clang! Clang!*

The blows were rhythmical, and there was a perceptible interval between each one and the next; they were drawn out and intolerably slow, and seemed to have lasted through uncountable eons.

It would be so easy to sink down into a deeper slumber, where even the clanging of the anvil beneath those hammer strokes would no longer be heard; but against this was the imperative need to save — not the world now, but — Jacqueline!

The remembrance freed me. Dimly, consciousness began to return. I knew the hammering was my own heart, forcing the blood heavily through the arteries of the brain.

That name — Annette — Jeannette — Jacqueline !

I had gone back to my rooms and saw a body upon the floor. Jacqueline had killed somebody, and I must save her!

All through the mist-wrapped borderland of life I heard her voice crying to me, her need of me dragging me back to consciousness. I struggled up out of the pit, and I saw light.

Suddenly I realized that my eyes were wide open and that I was staring at the moon over the housetops. With consciousness came pain. My head throbbed almost unbearably, and I was stiff with cold. I raised myself weakly, and then I became aware that somebody was bending over me.

It was a roughly dressed, rough-looking denizen of the low quarter into which I had strayed. His arms were beneath my neck, raising my head, and he was looking into my face with an expression of great concern upon his own good-natured one.

'I thought you were dead!' I could make out amid the stream of his dialect, but the remainder of his speech was beyond my understanding.

'Help me!' I muttered, reaching for his hand.

He understood the gesture, for he assisted me to my feet, and, after I had leaned weakly against the wall of a house for a minute or two, I found that I could stand unassisted. I looked round in bewilderment.

'Where am I?' I asked, still bound by that first memory of New York.

'In Sous-le-Cap, *m'sieur*,' answered the man.

I felt in my pocket for my watch and drew it out. It was strange that the men had not robbed me, but I suppose they had become terrified at their work and had run off. However, I did not think of that at the time. I think my action was an automatic one, the natural refuge for a perplexed man. But the sight of the time brought back my memory, and the events of the day rushed back into my mind.

It was a few minutes past eight. And

the boat sailed at nine. I must have lain stunned in Sous-le-Cap Street for an hour and a half, at least, and only the supreme necessity of awakening, realized through unconsciousness, had saved me from dying under the snows.

I found that I could walk, and having explained to the man that I wished to go to the *château*, was taken by him to the top of a winding road near at hand, from which I could see my destination at no great distance from me.

Dismissing my friendly guide, and sending him back rejoicing with liberal largesse, I hurried as quickly as I could make my way along the ramparts, past the frowning, ancient cannon skirting the park, until I burst into the *château* at half past the hour. I must have presented a dreadful spectacle, for my hair and collar were matted with blood, and I saw the guests stare and shrink from me. The clerk came toward me and stopped me at the entrance to the elevator.

'Where is Miss Hewlett?' I gasped.

'Didn't you meet her? She left here nearly an hour ago.'

I caught him by the arm, and I think he imagined that I was going to seize him by the throat also, for he backed away from me, and I saw a look of fear come into his eyes. The elevator attendant came running between us.

'Your friend — ' he began.

'My *friend*?' I cried.

'He came for her and said that you had met with an accident,' the clerk continued. 'She went with him at once. He took her away in a sleigh. I was sure that you had missed her when you came in.'

But already I was halfway across the hall and running for the door. I raced wildly across the court and toward the terrace.

The meaning of the scheme was clear. Jacqueline was on Captain Duhamel's boat, which sailed at nine. And only twenty minutes remained to me. If I had not had the good luck to meet Dubois — !

I must have noticed a clock somewhere during the minute that I was in the *château*, and though I had not been conscious of it, the after-image loomed before my eyes. As I ran now I could see a huge phantom clock, the dial marked with enormous Roman letters, and the hands moving with dreadful swiftness toward the hour of nine.

I had underestimated Leroux's shrewdness. He must have telegraphed instructions from New York before my train was out of the county, secured the boat, laid his plans during his journey northward, and had me struck down while Jacqueline was stolen from my care. And he had spared no details, even to enlisting the aid of Père Antoine.

If he had known that my destination was the same as his, he might have waited. But it was not the character of the man to wait, any more than it was to participate personally in his schemes. He worked through others, sitting back and pulling the strings, and he struck each blow on time.

I should have read him better. I had always dawdled. I trusted to the future, instead of acting. What chance had I against a mind like his? I was a novice at chess, pitting myself against a master at the game.

I must have been running aimlessly up and down the terrace, blindly searching for a road down to the lower town, for a man seized me by the sleeve, and I looked into the face of the hotel clerk again. He seemed to realize that more was the matter even than my appearance indicated, for he asked no questions, but apparently divined my movements.

'This way!' he said, and hurried me to a sort of subway entrance, and down a flight of steps. Before me I saw the turnstile which led to a cable railway. He paid my fare and thrust me into a car. A boy came to close the latticed door.

'Wait!' I gasped. 'Who was it that called?'

'The man with the mustache who asked for you — about whom you inquired.'

I turned away. I had thought it was Leroux. Of course it had not been he.

The car glided down the cliff and stopped a few seconds later. I emerged through another turnstile and found myself in the lower town again at the foot of the precipice, above which rose the *château* with its imposing façade, the ramparts, and the towering citadel. The hands of the phantom clock pointed to ten minutes of nine. But I knew the gulf lay before me at the end of the short, narrow street that led down to it, up which I had passed two hours before upon that journey which so nearly ended in the snow drifts of Sous-le-Cap.

I reached the wharf and raced along the planks. I was in time, although the engines were throbbing in the *Sainte-Vierge*. But it was not she, but the dark *Claire* I sought at that moment, and I dashed toward her.

A man barred my approach. He caught me in his strong arms and held me fast. I dashed my fists against his face, but he would not let me go.

'Are you mad, *monsieur*?' he burst out as I continued to struggle.

And then I recognized my captor as Captain Dubois. 'Jacqueline is on the *Claire*!' I cried, trying to make him understand. 'They took her there. They — '

'It is all right,' answered Dubois, holding me with one hand, while with the other he wiped a blood drop from his lip where I had struck him. 'It is all right. I have her.'

I stared wildly at him. 'She is on the *Claire*!' I cried again.

'No, *mon ami*. She is aboard the *Sainte-Vierge*' replied Dubois, chuckling. 'And if you wish to accompany *mademoiselle*, you must come with me at once, for we are getting up steam.'

I could not believe him. I thought that Leroux had tampered with the honest man. It was not until he had taken me half-forcibly aboard, and opened the cabin door, that I saw her. She was seated upon her berth, and she rose and came toward me with a glad little cry.

'*Jacqueline*!' I cried, and clasped her in my arms for joy, and quite forgot.

A dancing shadow fell upon the wall behind the oil lamp. The honest captain was rubbing his hands in the doorway and chuckling with delight.

'It is all right, it is all right; excuse me, *monsieur*?' he said, and closed the door on us. But I called him, and he returned, not very reluctantly.

'What has happened, Captain?' I asked.

'You are not going to leave me in suspense?'

'But what has happened to *you*, *monsieur*?' he asked, with great concern, as he saw the blood on my coat collar. 'You have met with an accident?'

Jacqueline cried out and ran for water, and made me sit down, and began bathing my head. I contrived to whisper something of what had occurred during the moments when Jacqueline flitted to and fro. Dubois swore roundly.

'It is my fault, *monsieur*,' he said. 'I should have known. I should have accompanied you home. It would be a tough customer who would venture to meddle with Alfred Dubois! But I was anxious to get to the telegraph office to inform M. Danton of your coming. And I suspected something, too, for I knew that Leroux had something more in his mind than simply to convey some of his men to St. Boniface at such expense.

'So as soon as I had finished telegraphing I hurried home and bade adieu to Marie and the little Madeline and the two nephews, and then I came back to the boat — and that part I shall tell you later, for *mademoiselle* knows nothing of the plot against her, and has been greatly distressed for you. So it shall be understood that you fell down and hurt your head on the ice — eh?'

I agreed to this. 'But what did she think?' I asked as Jacqueline went back for some more water.

'That you had sent her to the *Sainte-Vierge*,' he answered, 'and that you were to follow her here — as you did. Even now the nephews are searching the lower town for you.'

'But if I had not come before nine?'

'I should have waited all night, *monsieur*, even though I had lost my post for it,' he said explosively, and I reached out and gripped his hand. 'You may not have seen the baggage here,' continued the captain slyly.

I glanced round me. Upon the floor stood the two suitcases, which should have been in our rooms in the *château*, and Jacqueline was busily tearing up some filmy material in hers for bandages. I looked at Dubois in astonishment.

'Ah, *monsieur*, I sent for those,' he said, 'and paid your bill also. When I fight Simon Leroux, I do not do things by halves. You see, *monsieur*, wise though he is, there are other minds equal to his own, and since he killed my brother, I — '

Here he nearly broke down, and I looked discreetly away.

'One question of curiosity, *monsieur*, if it is permissible,' he said a little later. 'Why does Leroux wish so much to stop your marriage with *mademoiselle* that he is ready to stoop to assassination and kidnapping?'

My heart felt very warm toward the good man. I knew how that loose end in the romance that he had built up troubled him. And, though I hardly knew myself, I must give him some satisfactory solution of his problem.

'Because he is himself in love with her,' I said.

The captain clenched his fists. 'God forbid!' he muttered. 'They say his wife died of a broken heart. Ah, *monsieur*, swear to me that this shall never come about, that *mademoiselle* become his wife. Swear it to me, *mon ami*!'

I swore it, and we shook hands again. I was sorry for my deception then, and afterward I had occasion to remember it.

Five minutes later we had cast off, and the *Sainte-Vierge* steamed slowly through the drift ice that packed the gulf. There were no lights upon the *Claire*, and I surmised that the conspirators were keeping quietly hidden in expectation of Jacqueline's arrival, though how Dubois had outwitted them I could not at the time surmise. However, there was little doubt that once the trick was discovered, the *Claire* would follow on our heels.

Standing on deck, I watched the lights of Levis and Quebec draw together as we steamed eastward. I cast a last look at the *château* and the ramparts. I felt it would be many days before I set eyes on them again.

Then I sought my cabin and fell asleep, dreaming of Jacqueline.

8

Dreams of the Night

Jacqueline and I were together, the only human beings within a score of miles. We were seated side by side in the sleigh at which the dogs pulled steadily.

We glided with slow, easy monotony along the snow-covered trail, through the sparse forest that fringed the ice-bound waters of the Rivière d'Or. Seen through our tinted snow-glasses, the landscape was a vast field of palest blue, dotted with scattered clusters of spruce and pine trees.

The mystery of Jacqueline's rescue by Captain Dubois had been a simple one. The young man with the moustache was a certain Philippe Lacroix, well known to Dubois, a member of a good family, but of dissolute habits — just such a one as Leroux found it convenient to attach to his political fortunes by timely financial aid. Having acquired power over him, Leroux was in this way enabled to obtain political influence through his family connections. There was no doubt that he had been in New York with Leroux, and that they had hatched the plot to kidnap Jacqueline after I had been struck down.

Fortunately for us, Lacroix, ignorant, as was Leroux himself, that the two ships had exchanged roles and duties, took Jacqueline aboard the *Sainte-Vierge*, where Captain Dubois, who was waiting in anticipation of just such a scheme, seized him and marched him at pistol point to the house on Paul Street, in which Lacroix was kept a prisoner by friends of Dubois until the *Sainte-Vierge* had sailed.

The gulf was fairly free from ice, and our journey to St. Boniface, where we arrived on the fifth morning after our departure from Quebec, had been an uneventful one. We had not seen the smoke of the *Claire* behind us at any period during the voyage, and Dubois had not spared his coal to show the other vessel his heels. He left us at St. Boniface with a final caution against Leroux, and proceeded along the shore with his bags of mail; but first he had a satisfactory conversation with M. Danton concerning us.

I had given Dubois to understand that Jacqueline had been ill. I was apprehensive that he might question her and so discover her mental state; but the good man readily understood that an elopement causes much mental anguish in the case of the feminine party — at least this supposition was in line with the romantic books that the captain had read; and he leaped at the hypothesis. He not only forbore to question Jacqueline, but he explained the situation to Danton, a friendly but taciturn old man who kept the store and post office at St. Boniface.

Danton, who of course knew Jacqueline, took the opportunity of assuring me that her father, though a recluse and a misanthrope who had not left his seigniory for forty years, was said to be a man of heart, and would undoubtedly forgive us. He was clearly under the impression that we were married, and, since Dubois had not enlightened him on this point, I did not do so.

In fact, his ignorance again aroused in me elusive hopes — for if a marriage had occurred, would he not have known of it? At any rate, I should know soon; and with this reflection I had to console myself.

Since Jacqueline was supposed to know the route, I could ask no direct questions; but I gathered that the *château* lay about a hundred and twenty miles northwestward. For the first part of the journey we were to travel along the right bank of the Rivière d'Or; at the point where the mountains began there were some trappers' huts, and there doubtless I could gain further information.

M. Danton had his sleigh and eight fine-looking dogs ready for us. I purchased these outright in order to carry no hostages. We took with us several days' supply of food, a little tent, sleeping bags, and frozen fish for the animals.

I must record that a small wharf was in course of construction, and that the contractor's sign read: 'Northern Exploitation Company'. M. Danton informed me that this was a lumber company which had already begun operations, and that the establishment of its camps accounted for the absence of inhabitants. In fact, our arrival was almost unobserved, and two hours afterward we had set forth upon our journey.

I wondered what Jacqueline remembered. Vague and unquiet thoughts seemed to float up into her mind, and she sat by my side silent and rather sad. I think she was afraid of the knowledge that was to come to her. For this reason I resolved to ask no questions unless they should become necessary. Whether or not she even knew the route, I had no means of discovering.

The sun shone brightly; the air, intensely cold, chilled our faces, but could not penetrate our furs. Sometimes we rubbed each other's cheeks with snow when they grew threateningly white, laughing to see the blood rush to the under surface of the skin, and jested about our journey to drive away our fears. And it was wonderful. It was as though we were the first man and woman in the world, wandering in our snow-garden, and still lost in amazement at each other. The prospect of meeting others of our kind began to be a fantastic horror to me.

We were happy with each other. I watched her beautiful, serene face; the brown hair, brought low over the ears to guard them against the cold; the big grey eyes that were turned upon mine sometimes in puzzled wonder, but very real content. I held her small gloved hand inside the big sable muff, and we would sit thus for hours in silence while the dogs picked their way along the trail. When I looked back, I could see the tiny pad-prints stretching away toward the far horizon, an undeviating black blur upon the whiteness of the snow.

It was a strange situation. It might easily have become an impossible one. But it was a sacred comradeship, refined above the love of friend for friend, or lover for lover, by her faith, her helplessness, and need.

When we had fed the dogs at noon and eaten our meal, we would strap on the *raquettes*, the snow shoes with which

Danton had furnished us, and travel over the crusted drifts beside the stream. We ran out on the surface of the river and made snowballs, and pelted each other, laughing like school children. But after the journey had begun once more, we would sit quietly beside each other, and for long we would hardly utter a word. I think that she liked best to sit beside me in the narrow sleigh and lean against my shoulder, her physical weariness the reflection of her spiritual unrest. She did not want to think, and she wanted me to shield her. But even in this solitude fear drove me on, for I knew that a relentless enemy followed hard after us, camping where we had camped and reading the miles between us by the smouldering ashes of our old fires. At nightfall I would pitch the tent for Jacqueline and place her sleeping bag within, and while she slept I would lie by the huge fire near the dogs, and we kept watch over her together. So passed three days and nights.

The fourth short day drew toward its end a little after four o'clock. I remember that we camped late, for the sun had already dipped to the level horizon and was casting black mile-long shadows across the snow. A whistling wind came up. The dogs had been showing signs of distress that afternoon, pulling us more and more reluctantly, and walking with drooping ears and muzzles depressed.

I hammered in the pegs and built a fire with dry boughs, collecting a quantity of wood sufficient to last until morning. Then Jacqueline made tea, and we ate our supper and crept into our sleeping bags and lay down.

'Three more days, dear, at most, and our journey and our troubles will all be at an end,' I had said. 'Let us be happy together while we have each other, and when our mutual need is past I shall stay with you until you send me away.'

'That will never be, Paul,' she answered simply. 'But I shall be happy with you while our day lasts.'

And I thought of the text: 'For soon the long night cometh.'

I lay outside the tent, trying to sleep; but could not still my mind. The uncertainty ahead of us, the knowledge of

Leroux behind, tried me sorely, and only Jacqueline's need sustained my courage.

As I was on the point of dropping asleep, I heard a lone wolf howl from afar, and instantly the pack took up the cry. One of the dogs, a great tawny beast who led them, crept toward me and put his head down by mine, whimpering. The rest roamed ceaselessly about the fire, answering the wolf's challenge with deep wolf-like baying.

I drew my pistols from the pockets of my fur coat. It was pleasant to handle them. They gave me assurance. We were two fugitives in a land where every man's hand might be against us, but at least I had the means to guard my own. And looking at them, I began to yield to that temptation which had assailed me ceaselessly, both at Quebec and since we left St. Boniface, not to yield up Jacqueline, never to let her go.

Jacqueline glided out of the tent and knelt beside me, putting her arms about the dog's neck and her head upon its furry coat. The dogs loved her, and she seemed always to understand their needs.

'Paul, there is something wrong with them,' she said, her hand still caressing the mane of the great beast, who looked at her with pathetic eyes. I had noticed that they did not eat that night, but had imagined that they would do so later when they had recovered from their fatigue.

'What is wrong with them, Jacqueline?' I asked.

She raised her head and looked sadly at me. 'It is I, Paul,' she answered.

'You, Jacqueline?'

'Yes, it is *I*!' she cried with sudden, passionate vehemence. 'It is *I* who am *wrong* and have brought trouble on you. Paul, I do not even know how you came into my life, nor who I am, nor *anything* that happened to me at any time before you brought me to Quebec, except that my home is there.' She pointed northward. 'Who am I? Jacqueline, you say. The name means nothing to me. I am a woman without a past or future, a shadow that falls across your life, Paul. And I could perhaps remember, but I know — *I know* — that I must *never remember*.'

109

She began weeping wildly.

I surmised that she must have been under an intense strain for days. I had not dreamed that this woman who walked by my side and paid me the tribute of her docile faith suffered and knew.

I took her hand in mine. 'Jacqueline, it is best to forget these things until the time comes to remember them. It will come. Let us be happy till then. You have been ill, and you have had great trouble. That is all. I am taking you home. Do you not remember anything about your home, Jacqueline?'

She clapped her hands to her head and gave a little terrified cry. 'I — think — so,' she murmured. 'But I dare not remember, Paul. I have dreamed of things,' she went on in agitated, rapid tones, 'and then I have seemed to remember everything. But when I wake I have forgotten, and it is because I know that I must forget. Paul, I dream of a dead man, and men who hate and are following us. Was there — ever — a dead man, Paul?' she asked, shuddering.

'No, dear Jacqueline,' I answered

stoutly. 'Those dreams are lies.'

She still looked hopelessly at me, and I knew she was not quite convinced.

'Jacqueline, there never was any dead man,' I said. 'It is not true. Someday I will tell you everything — someday — ' I broke off helplessly, for my voice failed me, I was so shaken. I knew that at last I was conquered by the passion that possessed me, long repressed, but not less strong for its repression. I caught her in my arms. 'I love you, Jacqueline!' I cried. 'And you — you?'

She thrust her hands out and turned her face away. There was an awful fear upon it. 'Paul,' she cried, 'there is — somebody — who . . . I have known that,' she went on in a torrent of wild words. 'I have known that always, and it is the most terrible part of all!'

I laid a finger on her lips. 'There is nobody, Jacqueline,' I said again, trying to control my trembling voice. 'He was another delirium of the night, a phantom of your illness, dear. There was never anybody but me, and there shall never be. For tomorrow we shall turn back toward

St. Boniface again, and we shall take the boat for Quebec — and from there I shall take you to a land where there shall be no more grief, neither — ' I broke off suddenly. What had I said? My words — why, the devil had been quoting scripture again! The bathos of it! My sacred task forgotten and honour thrown to the winds, and Jacqueline helpless there! I hung my head in misery.

'Paul, dear, if there never was anyone — if it is nothing but a dream — ' Here she looked at me with doubtful scrutiny in her eyes, and then hastened to make amends for doubting me. 'Of course, Paul, if there had been, you could not have known. But though I know my heart is free — if there was nobody — why, let us go forward to my father's home, because there will be no cause there to separate us. So let us go on.'

'Yes, let us go on,' I muttered dully. But when the issue came, I knew that I would let no man stand between us.

'And someday I am going to tell you everything I know, and you shall tell me,' she said. 'But tonight we have each other, and will not think of unhappy things — nor ever till the time comes.'

She leaned back against my shoulder and held out her hands to the fire light. She had taken off her left glove, and now again I saw the wedding ring upon her finger.

She was asleep. I drew her head down on my knees and spread my coat around her, and let her rest there. She was happy again in sleep, as her nature was to be always. But, though I held her as she held my heart, my soul seemed dead, and I waited sleepless and heard only the whining of the heavy wind and scurry of the blown snow.

The wolf still howled from afar, but the dogs only whimpered in answer among the trees, where they had withdrawn.

At last I raised her in my arms and carried her inside the tent. She did not waken, but only stirred and murmured my name drowsily. I stood outside the tent and listened to her soft breathing. How helpless she was! How trusting! That turned the battle. Never again dare I breathe a word of love to her so long as that shadow obscured her mind. But if sunlight succeeded shadow . . .

The fire had sunk to a heap of red-grey ashes. I piled on fresh boughs till the embers caught flame again and the bright spears danced under the pines. The reek of smoking pine logs is in my nostrils yet.

9

The Fungus

My rest was miserable. In a succession of brief dreams, I fled with Jacqueline over a wilderness of ice, while in the distance, ever drawing nearer, followed Leroux, Lacroix, and Père Antoine. I heard Jacqueline's despairing cries as she was torn from me, while my weighted arms, heavier than lead, drooped helplessly at my sides, and from afar Simon mocked me.

Then ensued a world without Jacqueline, a dead eternity of ice and snow.

I must have fallen sound asleep at last, for when I opened my eyes the sun was shining brightly low down over the Rivière d'Or. The door of the tent stood open and Jacqueline was not inside.

With the remembrance of my dream still confusing reality, I ran toward the trees, shouting for her in fear. 'Jacqueline! Jacqueline!' I called.

She was coming toward me. She took me by the arm. 'Paul!' she began with quivering lips. 'Paul!'

She led me into the recesses of the pines. There, in a little open place, clustered together upon the ground, were the bodies of our dogs. All were dead, and the soft forms were frozen into the snow, which the poor creatures had licked in their agony, so that their open jaws were stuffed with icicles.

Jacqueline sank down upon the ground and sobbed as though her heart would break. I stood there watching, my brain paralyzed by the shock of the discovery.

Then I went back to the sleigh, on the rear of which the frozen fish was piled. I noticed that it had a faint, slightly aromatic odor. I flung the hard masses aside and scooped up a powdery substance with my hands.

Mycology had been a hobby of mine, and it was easy to recognize what that substance was. It was the *amanita*, the deadliest and the most widely distributed of the fungi, and the direst of all vegetable poisons to man and beast alike. The alkaloid which it contains takes effect only some hours after its ingestion, when it has entered the bloodstream and begun its disintegrating action upon the red corpuscles. The dogs must have partaken of it on the preceding afternoon.

Jacqueline joined me. The tears were streaming down her cheeks; she slipped her arm through mine and looked mutely at me.

I knew this was Leroux's work. He had tricked me again. I had seen clusters of the frozen fungus outside St. Boniface. I suppose that, when winter comes suddenly, such growths remain standing till spring thaws and rots them, retaining in the meanwhile all their noxious qualities. It would have been an easy matter for one of Leroux's agents to have cast a few handfuls of the deadly powder over the fish while the sleigh stood waiting outside Danton's door, and the jolting of the vehicle would have shaken the substance down into the middle of the heap, so that it would be three or four days before the dogs got to the poisoned fish.

I was mad with anger. The white landscape seemed to swim before my eyes. I meant to kill the man now, and without mercy. I would be as unscrupulous as he. He would be in this place by the afternoon; I would wait for him outside the trail. My pistols —

Jacqueline was looking up into my face in terror. The sight of her recalled me to my senses. Leroux afterward — first my duty to her!

'Paul! What is the matter, Paul?' she cried. 'I never saw you look like that before.'

I calmed myself and led her away, and presently we were standing before the fire again. 'Jacqueline,' I said, 'it is easier to go on than to turn back now.'

She watched me like a lip-reader. 'Yes, Paul; let us go on,' she answered.

So we went on. But our journey was to be very different now. There was no possibility of taking much baggage with us. We took a few things out of our suitcases and disposed them about us as best we could. The heavy sleeping bags would have made our progress, encumbered as we were with our fur coats, too slow; but I had hopes that we would reach the trappers' huts that afternoon, and so decided to discard them in favour of the fur-lined sleigh-rug, which would at least keep Jacqueline warm.

So we strapped on our snow shoes, and I made a pack and put three days' supplies of food in it and fastened it on my shoulders, securing it with two straps from the harness. I rolled the rug into a bundle and tied it below the pack; and thus equipped, we left the dead beasts and the useless sleigh behind us for Leroux's satisfaction, and set out briskly upon our march.

It is a strange thing, but no sooner had I passed out of sight of the sleigh than, weighted though I was, I felt my spirits rising rapidly. The freedom of movement and the exhilarating air gave my mind a new sense of liberty.

The cold was less intense, but, looking at the sky, which was heavily overcast, I knew that the rise in temperature betokened the advent of a heavy fall of snow, probably before night.

We stopped to look at the trees and the traces of deer-cropping upon the bark. Sometimes we took to the river-bed, and then again we paced among the trees, which were now becoming so sparsely scattered that the trail was hardly discernible. This caused me no concern, however, for I believed that when we reached the huts, we should be able to obtain certain information as to the remainder of our course.

We must have covered at least a dozen miles or more at the time, when we stopped for a brief midday meal. I was a little fatigued from carrying the pack, and my ankles ached from the snow shoes; but Jacqueline, who had evidently been accustomed to their use, was as fresh as when she started. I was glad of the respite; but we needed to press on. It was probable that Simon would camp by our dismantled sleigh that night.

When we resumed our march the character of the country began to change. Hitherto we had been traversing an almost interminable plain, but now a ridge of jagged mountains, bare at their peaks and fringed around the base with evergreens, appeared in the distance. The sky became more leaden.

Suddenly we emerged from among the trees upon an almost barren plateau, and there again we halted for a breathing spell. All that morning I had been looking for the trappers' huts. I had already come to the conclusion that M. Danton's instructions were to be taken by and large, for we could not now be more than twenty-five miles from the *château*, and it was only here that the Rivière d'Or left us, whirling in quick cascades, ice-free, among the rocks of its narrow bed, some distance east of us.

There was, of course, the possibility that the distance had been understated, and that we were only now halfway. But I could not let my mind dwell upon that possibility.

I scanned the horizon on every side. It had seemed to me all that day that our road was running uphill; but now, looking back, I was astonished to see how high we had ascended, for the whole of the vast plain across which we had been travelling lay spread out like a wrinkled tablecloth before my eyes.

In that grey light, which shortened

every distance, it almost seemed that I could discern the slope of the St. Lawrence far away, and the hills, foot-spurs of the mighty Laurentian range that bordered it. The mountains which we were approaching seemed quite near, and I knew that beyond them lay the seigniory.

I resolved to take my bearings still more accurately, and telling Jacqueline to wait for me a few minutes at the base of a hill and setting down my pack, I began the ascent alone. The climb was longer than I had anticipated. My eyes were aching from the glare of the snow. I had left my coloured glasses behind me in the tent and gone on, saying nothing, though I had realized my loss when I was only a mile or so away. However, I hoped that the night would restore my sight, and so, dismissing the matter from my mind, I struggled up until at last I stood upon the summit of the hill.

The view from this point was a stupendous one. New peaks sprang into vision, shimmering in the sunlight. Patches of dark forest stained the whiteness of the land, and far away, like a thin winding ribbon among the hills, I saw the valley of the Rivière d'Or. I gasped in delight and lingered to enjoy the grandeur of the spectacle.

Beneath me I saw Jacqueline waiting, a tiny figure upon the snow. My heart smote me with a deep sense of reproach that I had put her to so much sacrifice. But I had seen the valley between those mountains, the only possible entrance to that mysterious land. Nothing could fail us now.

I cast my eyes beyond her toward the mist-wrapped tops of the far Laurentians and the plains. And a sense of an inevitable fate came over me as I perceived far away a tiny crawling ant upon the snows — Simon Leroux's dog sleigh . . .

I went back to the little patient figure that was waiting for me, and I took up my pack again and told her nothing. She stepped bravely out beside me, frozen, fatigued, but willing because I bade her. She did not ask anything of me.

The sun dipped lower, and far away I

heard the howl of the solitary wolf again. My mind had been working very fast during that journey down the hill, and long before I reached Jacqueline I had resolved that she should know nothing of the pursuit until the moment came when she must be told.

That the pursuer was Leroux there could be no possible doubt. He had evidently passed the sleigh, and was undoubtedly pressing forward, elated and confident of our capture. But he must still be at least a dozen miles away. He could not reach us that night, and he could hardly travel by night. We should have a half-day's start of him in the morning.

I gripped my pistols as we strode along. We went on and on. The afternoon was wearing away; the sun was very low now and all its strength had gone. The wolf followed us, howling from afar. Once I saw it across the treeless wastes — a gaunt white dog-like figure trotting against the steely grey of the sky. We ascended the last of the foothills before the trail dipped toward the valley, which was guarded by two sentinel mountains of that jagged ridge before us. From the top I looked back. Simon was nowhere to be seen.

'Courage, Jacqueline,' I said, patting her arm. 'The huts ought to be here.'

Her courage was greater than my own. She looked up and smiled at me. And so we descended and went on, and the sun dipped below the edge of the world.

The wolf crept nearer, and its howls rang out with piercing strokes across the silence. My eyes ached so that I could hardly discern the darkening land, and the snow came down, not steadily, but in swirling eddies blown on fierce gusts of wind.

And suddenly raising my eyes despairingly, I saw the huts. They stood about four hundred yards away from where the trail ran through the mountains. There were five of them, and they had not been occupied for at least two seasons, for the blackened timbers were falling apart, and the roofs had been torn off all but one of them, no doubt for fuel. The wind was whirling the snow wildly around them, and it whistled through the broken, rotting walls.

I flung my pack inside the roofed one and began tearing apart the timbers of another to make a fire. Jacqueline stood looking at me in docile faith.

'I can go on,' she said quietly. 'I can go on, Paul.'

I caught her hands in mine. 'We shall stay here, Jacqueline,' I said.

She did not answer me, but, opening the pack, began the preparation of our meal, which consisted of some biscuits left from the night before, when we had made a quantity on the wood ashes. We made tea over the roaring flames, and sat listening to the wolf's call and the wind that drove our fire in gusts of smoke and flame.

The wind grew fiercer. It was a hurricane. It drowned the wolf's call; it almost silenced the sound of our own voices. Thank God that we had at least our shelter in that storm.

I scooped out a bed for Jacqueline inside the snow-filled hut and spread it with the sleigh robe. She lay down in her fur coat, and I wrapped the ends around her. I looked into her sweet face and marveled at its serenity. Her eyes closed wearily.

But, though I was as tired as she, I could not sleep. I crouched over the fire, pondering over the morrow's acts. Should I wait for Leroux and shoot him down like a dog if he molested us? Or should we hide among the hills and watch him pass by? But that would avail us nothing. If we went on, we must encounter him, and the sooner the better.

This problem and a fiercer one filled my mind, for my soul was as storm-beset as the hut, whose planking shook under the gale's force. I realized how incongruous my position was.

I had no status at all. I was accompanying a runaway wife back to her father's home, perhaps to meet her husband there. And whether Leroux held me in his present power or not, inexorably I was heading for his own objective.

10

Snow Blindness

More madly now than ever, I felt that fierce temptation. There she lay, the one woman who had ever seriously come into my life, sleeping so near to me that I could bend down and rest my hand on the inert form over which the snow drifted so steadily.

I brushed it away. I brooded over her. Why had I ever brought her on that journey? If I had taken her to Jamaica, where I had planned to go, instead of engaging that mock-heroic odyssey — there, among palm trees, in an eternal spring, there would have been no need that she should remember.

I looked down on her. Again the snow covered her.

It fell so inexorably. It was like Leroux. It was as tireless as he, and as implacable as he. I brushed it away with frantic haste, and still it drifted into the doorless hut.

A dreadful fear held me in its grip: what if she never awoke? Some people died thus in the snow. I raised the sleigh robe, and saw that the fur coat stirred softly as she breathed.

At last, out of the wild passions that fought within me, decision was born. I would be ready for Leroux, and let him act as he saw fit. I loaded my pistols. I could do no more than fight for Jacqueline. And with that determination I grew calm. And I sat over the fire and let my imagination stray toward some future when our troubles would be in the past and we should be together.

'Paul!'

I must have been half-asleep, for I came back to myself with a start and sprang to my feet. Jacqueline had risen upon her knees; she flung her arms out wildly, and suddenly she caught her breath and screamed, and stood up, and ran uncertainly toward me, with hands that groped for me. She found me; I caught her, and she pushed me from her and shuddered and stared at me in that uncertain doubt that follows dreams.

'I am here, Jacqueline,' I said. 'With you — always, till you send me away.' She knew me not, and she was recoiling from me, out through the hut door, into the blinding snow. I sprang after her. 'Jacqueline! It's me — Paul! *Jacqueline!*'

She was running from me and screaming in the snow. I heard her moccasins breaking through the thin ice crust. And, mad with terror, I rushed after her.

And as I emerged from the hut's shelter, a red-hot glare from the east seemed to sear and kill my vision. It was the rising sun. I had thought it night, and it was already day. And I could see nothing through my swollen eyelids except the white light of the shining snow. The wind howled round me, and though the sun shone, the snowflakes stung my face like hail.

I did not know under the influence of what dread dream she was. But I ran wildly to and fro, calling her, and now and again I heard the sound of her little moccasins as she plunged through the knee-high snow. Once I heard her panting breath behind me; but I never caught her.

And never once did she answer me.

'What is it? What is it?' I pleaded madly. 'Jacqueline, don't you know me? Don't you remember me?'

The sound of the moccasins far away, and then the whine of the wind again. I did not know where the huts were now. I could see nothing but a yellow glare. And fear of Leroux came on me and turned my heart to water. I stood still, listening, like a hunted stag. There came no sound.

It was horrible, in that wild waste, alone. I tried to gather my scattered senses together.

Eastward, I knew the river lay, and that blinding brightness came from the east. Southward a little distance was the hill that we had last ascended on the evening before. I could discern the merest outlines of the land, but I fancied that I could see that it sloped upward toward the south.

I set off in the direction of the hill, and soon I found myself climbing. The elevation hid the sun, and this enabled me to glimpse my surroundings dimly, as through a heavy veil.

I called once more, and then I was scrambling up the hill, stumbling and falling on the ice-coated boulders. My coat was open, and the wind cut like a knife-edge, but I did not notice it. Perhaps from the hilltop I should see her.

'Jacqueline! *Jacqueline!*' I screamed frantically. No answer came.

I had gained the summit now, and round me I saw the shadowy outlines of the snow-covered rocks, but five or six feet from me a deep, impenetrable grey wall obscured everything. I tried to peer down into the valley, and saw nothing but the same fog there. Once more I called.

A dog barked suddenly, not far away, and through the mist I heard the slide of sleigh-runners on snow; and then I knew. I scrambled down, slipping and gashing my hands upon the rocks and ice. At the foot of the hill I saw two straight and narrow lines on the soft snow. They were the tracks of sleigh-runners.

I followed them, sobbing, and catching my breath, and screaming: 'Jacqueline! *Jacqueline!*'

Then I heard Simon's voice, and with

the sound of it my dream came back with prophetic clearness.

'*Bonjour*, M. Hewlett!' he called mockingly. 'This way! This way!'

I turned and rushed blindly in the direction of the cry. I had left my snow shoes behind me in the hut, and at each step my feet broke through the crusted snow, so that I floundered and fell like a drunken man to choruses of taunts and laughter. It was a horrible blindman's bluff, for they had surrounded me, yelling from every quarter.

'This way, *monsieur* This way!' piped a thin voice which I knew to be Philippe Lacroix.

A snowball struck me on the chin, and they began pelting me and laughing. I was like a baited bear. I was beside myself with rage and helpless fury. The icy balls hit my face a dozen times; one struck me behind the ear and hurled me down, half-stunned.

I was up again and rushing at my unseen tormentors. I heard the barking of the dogs far away, and I ran in the direction of the sound, sobbing with rage.

I pulled my pistols from my pockets and spun round, firing in every direction through that wall of grey, yielding mist that gave me place but never gave me vision.

The clouds had obscured the sky and the snow was falling again. My hands were bare and numb, except where the cold steel of the pistol triggers seared my fingers like molten metal.

They had formed a wider circle round me, and pistol range is longer than snowball range, so that they struck me no more. I heard the shouts and mockery still, but never Jacqueline's voice.

'Here, M. Hewlett, here!' piped Philippe Lacroix once more.

Again I turned and rushed at him, firing shot after shot. I heard his snow shoes plodding across the crust, and yells from the others indicated that Philippe's adventure had been a risky one.

Then Simon called again and I turned, like a foolish baited beast, and fired at him.

A dog barked once more, very far away, and at last I understood their scheme.

Doubtless Simon had reached the huts at dawn and had discovered us there. He must have been in waiting, but when he saw Jacqueline run from me he changed his plans and sent the sleigh after her. Then, realizing from my actions that I was snow-blind, he had remained behind with some of his followers to enjoy the sport of baiting me, and incidentally to drive me out of the way while the sleigh went on.

And now there was complete silence. He had accomplished his purpose. He had gained all that he had to gain. Fortune had fought upon his side, as always.

But Jacqueline — She had tried to escape *me*. She could not have been playing a part — she was too transcendentally sincere. Something must have occurred — some dream which had momentarily crazed her; and she had confounded me with her persecutors.

I could not think evil of her. For her sake, I resolved to pull myself together. I did not now know whether Leroux was in front or behind me, or upon either hand.

I stood deep in the snow, a pistol in each hand, waiting. When he called again, I should make my last effort.

But he called me no more.

Once I heard the dog yelp, far up the valley, and then there was only the soughing of the wind and the sting of the driving sleet flakes. And the grey mist had closed in all about me. I was alone in that storm-swept wilderness and there was no sun to guide me.

I saw a shadow at my feet, and stooping down, perceived that accident had brought me back to the sleigh tracks. From the direction in which the dog had howled, I judged that my course lay straight ahead as I was standing. I started off wearily. At least it was better to walk than to perish in the snow.

But before many minutes had passed, the realization of my loss stung me into madness again, and I began to run. And, as I ran, I shouted; and, shouting, I fired.

I plunged along — half-delirious, I believe, for I began to hear voices on every side of me and to imagine I saw Simon standing, just out of reach, a

136

shadow upon the mist, taunting me. I followed him at an undeviating distance, firing, reloading, and firing again. I was no longer conscious of my progress. The fingers that pressed the triggers of my pistols had no sensation in them, and in my imagination were parts of a monstrous mechanism which I directed. My legs, too, felt like stilts that somebody had strapped to my body. My mind drifted . . .

Somebody was shaking me . . .

'Get up!' he bellowed in my ear. 'Get up! Do you want to die in the snow?'

I closed my eyes and sank back into a lethargy of sleep.

11

The Château

I had an indistinct impression of being carried for what seemed an eternity upon the shoulders of my rescuer, and of clinging there through the delirium that supervened.

Sometimes I thought I was on a camel's back, pursuing Jacqueline's abductors through the hot sands of an Egyptian desert; sometimes I was on shipboard, sinking in a tropical sea, beneath which amid the marl and ooze of delta depositions, hideous, antediluvian creatures, with faces like that of Leroux, writhed and stretched up their tentacles to drag me down.

Then I would be conscious of the cold and bitter wind again. But at last there came a grateful sense of warmth and ease, followed by a period of blank unconsciousness.

When at last I opened my eyes, it was

late afternoon. Though they pained me, I could now see with tolerable distinctness. I was lying upon a bed of dried balsam leaves inside a little hut, and through the half-open door I could see the sun just dipping behind the mountains. Besides the bed, the hut contained a roughly hewn table and chair and a bookcase with a few books in it. Upon a wall hung a big crucifix of wood, and under it an old man was standing.

He heard me stir and came toward me. I recognized the massive shoulders and commanding countenance of Père Antoine, and remembrance came back to me. 'Where am I?' I asked.

'In my cabin, *monsieur*,' answered the priest, standing at my side, an inscrutable calm upon his face.

'You saved me?'

'Three days ago. You were dying in the snow. You had fired off your pistols and had thrown your coat away. I had to carry you back and find it. It is lucky that I found you, *monsieur*, or assuredly you would soon have been dead. But for your dog — '

'*My* dog!' I exclaimed.

'Certainly, a dog came to me and brought me a mile out of my route to where you were lying. But, now, come to think of it, it disappeared and has not returned. Perhaps it was sent to me by *le bon Dieu*.'

'Where is Mlle. Duchaine?' I burst out.

'Ah, M. Hewlett,' said the priest, looking at me severely, 'that was a wild undertaking of yours, and God does not prosper such schemes, though I confess I do not understand why you were taking her to her home. Rest assured, she is in good hands. I met the sleigh containing her, and M. Leroux informed me that all would be well. It is strange that he did not speak of you, though, and I do not understand how — '

'He stole her from me when I was snow-blind, and left me to die!' I exclaimed. 'I must rescue her . . . '

Father Antoine laid a heavy hand upon my shoulder. 'Be assured, *monsieur*, that *madame* is perfectly happy and contented with her friends,' he said. 'And no doubt she has already regretted her escapade.

140

Did I not warn you in Quebec, *monsieur*, that your enterprise would be brought to naught? And now you will doubtless be glad of your lesson, and will abandon it willingly and return homeward. I have to depart at daybreak upon an urgent mission a hundred miles away, which was interrupted by your rescue; but I shall be back within a week, by which time you will doubtless be able to accompany me to the coast. Meanwhile, you will rest here, and my provisions and a few books are at your disposal.'

'I shall not!' I cried weakly. 'I am going on to the *château*!'

He looked at me steadily. 'You cannot,' he said. 'If you attempt it, you will perish by the way.'

'You cannot stop me!' I cried desperately.

'Perhaps not, *monsieur*; nevertheless, you will not be able to reach the *château*.'

'Who are you that you should stop me?' I exclaimed angrily. 'You are a priest, and your duty is with souls.'

'That is why,' answered Père Antoine. 'You are in pursuit of a married woman.'

'I do not know anything about that, but I am the protector of a defenceless one,' I answered, 'and I shall seek her until she sends me away. Do you know where her husband is?'

'No, *monsieur*,' answered the old man. 'And you?'

I burst into an impassioned appeal to him. I told him of Leroux and his conspiracy to obtain possession of the property, of my encounter with Jacqueline, and how I had rescued her, omitting mention of course of the murder. As I went on I could see the look of surprise upon his face gradually change into belief. I told him of our journey across the snow and begged him to help me to rescue Jacqueline, or at least to find her. I added that the trouble had partially destroyed her memory, so that she was not competent to decide who her protectors were.

When I had ended, he was looking at me with a benignancy that I had never seen before upon his face. 'M. Hewlett,' he answered, 'I have long suspected a part of what you have told me, and therefore I readily accept your statements. I believe now that *madame* has suffered no wrong from you. But I am a priest, and, as you say, my care is only that of souls. Madame is married. I married her — '

'To whom?' I cried.

'To M. Louis d'Epernay, nephew of M. Charles Duchaine by marriage, less than two weeks ago in the *château* here.'

The addition of the last word singularly revived my hopes. It had slipped from his lips unconsciously, but it gave me reason to believe that the *château* was nearby.

Father Antoine sat down upon the chair beside me. 'M. Duchaine has been a recluse for many years,' he said, 'and of late his mind has become affected. It is said that he was implicated in the troubles of 1867, and that, fearing arrest, he fled here and built this *château* in this desolate region, where he would be safe from pursuit. If anyone ever contemplated denouncing him, at any rate those events have long ago been forgotten. But solitude has made a hermit of him and taken him out of touch with the world of today.

'I believe that Leroux has discovered coal on his property, and by threatening him with arrest has gained a complete ascendency over the weak-minded old man. However, the fact remains that his daughter was married by me to M. d'Epernay some ten or twelve days ago at the *château*.

'I was uneasy, for it did not look to be like a love match, and I knew that M. d'Epernay had the reputation of a profligate in Quebec, where he was hand in glove with Philippe Lacroix, one of M. Leroux's aids. But a priest has no option when an expression of matrimonial consent is made to him in the presence of two witnesses. So I married them.

'My duties took me to Quebec. There I learned that Mme. d'Epernay had fled on the night of her marriage, and that her husband was in pursuit of her. Again it was told me that she was living at the *Château* Frontenac with another man. It was not for me to question whether she loved her husband, but to do my duty.

'I appealed to you. You refused to listen to my appeal. You threatened me, *monsieur*. And you denied my priesthood. However, I do not speak of that, for she is undoubtedly safe with her father now, awaiting her husband's return. And I shall not help you in your pursuit of her, M. Hewlett, for you are actuated solely by love for the wife of another man. Is that not so?' he ended, bending over me with a penetrating look in his blue eyes.

'Yes, it is so. But I shall go to the *château*,' I answered.

Père Antoine rose up. 'You will find food here,' he said, 'and if you wish to take exercise there are snow shoes. Try to find the *château* — do what you please; but remember that if you lose your way I shall not be here to save you. I shall return from my mission in a week and be ready to conduct you to St. Boniface. And now, *monsieur*, since we understand each other, I shall prepare the supper.'

I swallowed a few mouthfuls of food and fell asleep soon afterward. In the morning when I awoke the cabin was empty.

My eyes were almost well, but my hands had been badly frozen and were extremely painful, while I was so weak that I could hardly walk. I spent the next two days recovering my strength, and on the third I found myself able to leave the hut for a short tramp.

I found snow shoes and coloured glasses in the cabin; my overcoat was there, and I did not feel troubled in conscience when I appropriated a pair of warm fur mittens which the good priest had made from mink skins. They had no fingers, and were admirably adapted to the weather.

I found one of the pistols in the hut, and in the pocket of my fur coat were a couple of cartridges which I had over-looked. The rest I had fired away in my delirium.

The cabin was situated in a valley, around which high hills clustered. Strapping on the snow shoes, I set to work to climb a lofty peak which stood at no great distance.

It took me a couple of hours to make the ascent, and when at last I sank down exhausted on the summit there was nothing in sight but a succession of new hills in every direction. I seemed to be on the summit of the ridge which sloped away to east and west of me. Hidden among the hills were little lakes.

There was no sign of life in all that desolate country.

My disappointment was overwhelming. Surely the *château* was near. I strode up and down upon the mountaintop, clenching my hands with rage. It was four days since I had lost Jacqueline, and Leroux had contemptuously left me to die in the snow. He was so sure I could not follow and find him.

I began the descent again. But it is easy to lose one's way upon a mountain peak, and the hills presented no clear definition to me. Once in the valley I could locate the cabin again, but the sun had travelled far toward the west and no longer guided me accurately.

I must have turned off at a slight angle which took me some distance out of my course, for my progress was suddenly arrested by a mighty wall of rock, a sheer precipice that seemed to descend perpendicularly into the valley underneath.

Somewhere a torrent was roaring like a miniature Niagara.

I discovered my error and bent my footsteps along the summit of the precipice, and as I proceeded the noise of the torrent grew louder until the din was deafening. I was treading now upon a smooth slope. I continued the descent, and all at once, at no great distance from me, I saw a tremendous waterfall, ice-sheeted, that tumbled down the face of the declivity and sent up a cloud of misty spray.

I stopped to stare in admiration. Far below me the narrow valley had widened into the smooth snow-coated surface of a lake. And on a point of land projecting from the bottom of that mighty wall, I saw the *château*! It could have been nothing else. It was a splendid building — not larger than the house of a country gentleman, perhaps, and made of hewn logs; but the rude splendour of it against that icy, rocky background transfixed me with wonder.

It was a rambling, straggling building, apparently constructed at different times;

having two wings and a wide central hall, with odd projecting chambers, and it was hidden so cunningly away that it was visible from this side of the lake only from the point of the rocky precipice above on which I stood.

The *château* stood under the overhanging precipice in such a way that half the building was invisible even from here. It seemed to be set back into a hollow of the mountainside, which appeared every moment about to overwhelm it.

And now I perceived that the smooth slope on which I stood was a snow-covered glacier, a million tons of ice, pressing ever by its own weight toward the precipice, and carrying its debris of rocks and stones toward the waterfall that issued from it and poured in deafening clamour into the lake below. Where the precipice projected the waterfall was split in two, and rushed down in twin streams, bubbling, tumbling, hissing, plunging into the lake, which whirled furiously around the spit of land on which the castle stood, clear of ice for a distance of a hundred feet from the shore, a foaming maelstrom in which no boat that was ever built could have endured an instant, but must have been twisted and flung back like the fantastically shaped ice pinnacles along the marge.

On each side of the *château* a cataract plunged, veiling itself in an opacity of mist, tinted with all the spectral hues by the rays of the westering sun. I could have flung a stone down, not on the *château*, but over it, into the boiling lake. Why, that position was impregnable! Behind it the sheer precipice, up which not even a bird could walk; the impassable lake before it, and the torrent on either side!

But — how had M. Charles Duchaine gained entrance there? There seemed to be no entrance. And yet the *château* stood before my eyes, no dream, but very real indeed. There was a small piece of enclosed land between its front and the lake, and within this I thought I could see dogs lying.

That might have been my fancy, for the mountain was too high for me to be able to distinguish anything readily, and the sublime grandeur of the scene and the roar of the water made me incapable of clear discernment.

Before I reached the hut again, I had formulated my plan. I would start at dawn, or earlier, and work around these mountains, a circuit of perhaps twenty miles, approaching the *château* by the edge of the lake. I concluded that there must exist a ridge of narrow beach between the whirlpool and the castle, though it was invisible from above, and that the entrance would disclose itself to me in the course of my journey.

The hope of finding Jacqueline again banished the last vestiges of my weakness. I felt like one inspired. And my spirit was exalted, too. For she so completely filled my heart that she left no place for doubts and fears.

That night I paced the little cabin excitedly. And, as I paced it, suddenly I perceived a strange flicker of light in the north sky, and went to the door to see the most beautiful phenomenon that I had ever witnessed. There came first a flash, and swiftly long streamers of flame shot up and spread fanwise over the heavens.

They quivered and sank, and flared again, and broke into innumerable rippling waves; they hung, broad banners of light, athwart the skies, then slowly faded, to give place to a wavering interplay of ghostly beams that sought the darkest places beyond the moon: celestial fingers whiter than the white glow of a myriad of arc-lamps.

And somehow the wonder of it filled me with the conviction that all would be well. For those heavenly lights bridged the loneliness of my soul even as they bridged the sky from Jupiter, who blazed brilliant in the east to great Arcturus. And so I felt that, though I crossed a void as wide and fathomless in search of her, sometime she should be mine . . .

Although the sun was well above the horizon when I awoke, I started out on the fourth morning eager to achieve the entrance to the *château*. First I plodded back to the two mountains which guarded the approach to the valley, then worked round along the flank of the ridge of peaks, searching for an entrance. The further I went, however, the higher and more precipitous became the mountains.

I realized that there was little chance of finding any access along this side, so after my noon meal I ascended one of the lower elevations in order to obtain my bearings. But I could discern neither *château*, nor lake, nor waterfall; and the sound of the torrent far away to the left came to my ears only as a faint distant murmur. I was far out of the way.

The snow, which had been falling at intervals during each day since Jacqueline's abduction, had long ago covered up the tracks of the sleigh. I had to trust to my own wit to solve my problem, and there did not seem to be any solution. There was no visible entrance to that mountain lake on any side, and to descend that sheer ice-coated precipice was an impossibility.

It was long after nightfall when I reached the cabin again, exhausted and dispirited. I awoke too late on the fifth morning, and I was too stiff to make much of a journey. I climbed to the edge of the glacier once again in the hope of discovering an approach. I examined every foot of the ground with meticulous care.

But whenever I approached the edge, the same wall of rock ran down vertically for some three hundred feet, veneered with ice and wrapped in a perpetual blinding spray. And yet sleighs could enter that valley below. For at the extreme edge of the lake, outside the enclosed piece of land, I perceived one — a tiny thing far under me, and yet unmistakably a sleigh.

I was within three hundred feet of Jacqueline's home, and yet as far away as though leagues divided us. I looked down at the *château* and ground my teeth and swore that I would win her. But all the rest of that day went in fruitless searching.

I must succeed in finding the entrance on the following day, for now Père Antoine might return at any time, and I knew that he would prove far less tractable here in his own bailiwick than he had been when I defied him at the Frontenac. By hook or by crook I must gain entrance to the valley.

This was to be my last night in the cabin. I could not return, not though I were perishing in the snows. Happily my eyes were now entirely well, and my hands, though chapped and roughened from the frostbites, had suffered no permanent injury. So I started out with grim resolution on the sixth morning, when the dawn was only a red streak on the horizon and the stars still lit my way. Before the sun rose, I was standing once more outside those two sentinel peaks.

To this point I knew the sleigh had come. But whether it had continued straight down the valley or turned to the right along that same ridge which I had fruitlessly explored before, it was impossible to determine. I tried to put myself in the position of a man travelling toward the *château*. Which road would I take? How and where would it occur to me to seek an entrance into the heart of those formidable hills?

The more I puzzled and pondered over the difficulty, the harder it was to solve. As I stood, rather weary, balancing myself upon my snow shoes, I heard a wolf's howl quite near to me. Raising my head, I saw no wolf, but a familiar husky — the very dog I had encountered in New York, Jacqueline's dog!

12

Under the Mountains

The dog was standing on a rock at the base of the hill immediately before me — and I almost thought that it was calling me.

I took a few steps toward it, and it disappeared immediately, as though alarmed — apparently into the heart of the mountain. I thought, of course, that it was crouching in a hollow place, or behind a boulder, and would reappear on my approach, but when I reached the spot where it had been it was nowhere to be seen. And the paw-prints ran toward a tiny hole no bigger than the entrance to a fox's lair — and ended there.

At this spot an enormous boulder lay, almost concealing the burrow. I put my shoulder against it in the hope of dislodging it sufficiently to enable me to see into the cavity. To my astonishment, at the first

157

touch it rolled into a new position, disclosing a wide natural tunnel in the mountainside, through which a sleigh might have passed easily!

I saw at once the explanation. The boulder was a rocking stone. It must have fallen at some time from the top of the arch, and happened to be so poised that at a touch it could be swung into one of two positions, alternately disclosing and concealing the tunnel in the cliff wall.

I stepped within and, striking a match, perceived that I was standing inside a vast cave — a vaulted chamber that ran apparently straight into the heart of the mountains. Great stalactites hung from the roof and dripped water upon the floor, on which numerous small stalagmites were forming, where they had not been crumbled away by the passage and re-passage of sleighs. These had left two well-defined tracks in the soft stone under my feet.

The cave was one of those common formations in limestone hills. How far it ran I could not know, but I had little doubt that at last I was well upon my approach to the *château*. The interior was completely dark. At intervals I struck matches from the box which I had brought with me, but the road always ran clear and straight ahead, and I could even guide myself by the ruts in the ground. And every time I struck a match, I could see the vaulted cavern, wide as a great cathedral, extending right and left and in front of me.

I must have been journeying for half an hour when I perceived a faint light ahead of me, and at the same time I heard the gurgling of a torrent somewhere near at hand. The light grew stronger. I could see now that the cavern had narrowed considerably: there were no longer any ruts in the ground, and by stretching out my arms I could touch the wall on either side of me. I advanced cautiously until the light grew quite bright; I saw the tunnel end in front of me, and emerged into an open space in the heart of the hills.

I say an open space, for it was as large as two city blocks; but it was as though it had been dug out of the mountains by an enormous cheese scoop, for on all sides, sheer vertical walls of rock ascended, so high that the light of day filtered down only dimly. A swift river issuing from the base of one of these stupendous cliffs ran across the opening and disappeared into a cave upon the other side.

I glanced at my watch. It seemed that I had been travelling for an interminable time, but it was barely eleven o'clock. I sat down to eat, and the thought occurred to me that this would make a good camping place, if necessary, for it was quite warm at such a depth below the surface of the hills, and my fur coat had begun to feel oppressive. I felt drowsy, too, and somehow, before I was aware of any fatigue, I was asleep.

That was a lucky thing, for I was not destined to sleep much the following night. It was three o'clock when I awoke, and at first, as always since my journey began, I could not remember where I was. And, as always, it was the thought of Jacqueline that recalled to me my surroundings. I sprang to my feet and made hasty preparations to resume my journey.

A short investigation showed me that I had come into a cul-de-sac, for there was no path through the opposite hills. There were, however, a number of extensive caves in the porous limestone cliffs, any of which might prove to be the sequence of the road.

The first thing that I perceived on beginning my search was that men had been here before me. What was the place? A robbers' den? A camp of outlaws?

In the first cave that I explored, I found a stock of provisions — flour and canned meats and matches — snugly stored away safe from the damp and snow. Nearby were picks and shovels and three very reputable blankets, with a miscellany of materials suggestive of the camping party's outfit.

I might have been more surprised than I was, but my thoughts were centered on Jacqueline, and the waning of the light showed me that the sun must be well down in the sky. I must get on at once if I were to reach the *château* that night. But how?

I might have wandered for an indefinite

time among those caves before striking the road. That I was off the track now seemed certain, for it was obvious that no sleigh could pass through those walls. The thin drift of snow that had covered the ground was almost melted, but enough remained to have showed the paw-prints of the dog, if it had passed that way.

There was none; nor were there tracks of sleigh runners, which would at least have scored them in the sandy ooze along the bed of the rivulet. I had evidently then strayed from the right course while wandering through the tunnel, and thus come by mischance into this blind alley.

I had noticed, as I have said, that the path narrowed considerably during the last few hundred feet that I had traversed before I reached this open place. In the darkness I might easily have debouched along one of the numerous paths which, no doubt, existed all through the interior of this limestone formation.

I started back in haste and reentered the tunnel again, striking a match every few seconds, lighting each by its predecessor. I had been travelling back for about ten minutes when I noticed at my feet the charred stump of a match that I had thrown away some time before. I looked around me and saw that I was again in the main road. There were the faint depressions caused by the sleigh runners in the soft stone, and the roof and side walls of the tunnel again stretched away into the obscurity around me.

Satisfied that I had retraced my steps sufficiently far, I turned about and began to proceed cautiously in the opposite direction, keeping this time as far as possible to the right of the road instead of to the left, as before. The box of matches which I had brought with me was nearly exhausted, but, by shielding each one carefully, I was able to examine my ground with fair assurance of my being in the right course.

A draft was now beginning to blow quite strongly inward, and this convinced me that I was approaching the tunnel's end. As I proceeded, I kept looking to the left to endeavor to locate the narrow passage into which I had strayed; but it must have been the merest opening in the wall, so small that only a miracle of chance had led me into it, for I saw nothing but the straight passage before me.

Presently I began to hear a murmur of water in the distance, and then a faint flicker of light. The ground began to grow softer, and now I was treading upon ooze and mud instead of rock. The murmur increased in a sonorous crescendo until the full cadence of the mighty waterfall burst on my ears.

A fiery ball seemed to fill the exit. The red sun, barred with bands of coal-black cloud, was dipping into the farther verge of the lake.

The thunder of the cataracts filled my ears. A fine spray, like a garment of filmy silk, obscured my clearer vision; but through and beyond it, between two torrents that sailed above like crystal bows, I saw the *château* before me.

13

The Roulette-wheel

I stared at the scene in amazement, for the transition from the dark tunnel through which I had come was an astounding one, and I could hardly believe the evidence of my eyes. I had passed right through the hollow heart of those mighty hills and now stood underneath the huge glacier, with its million tons of ice above me, from which the cataracts tumbled, drenching me with spray, though I was fully a hundred yards away from the log *château*.

The building was located, as I had surmised, upon a narrow strip of land, invisible from above except where its tongue, containing the enclosed yard, ran out into the lake. It stood far back beneath the overhanging ledge and seemed to be secured against the living rock. It was evident that there was no other approach except the tunnel through which I had come, for all around the land that turbulent whirlpool raved, where the two cataracts contended for the mastery of the waters. And for countless ages they must have fought together thus, and neither gained, not since the day when those mountains rose out of the primeval ooze.

Within the enclosed space, which was larger than I had thought on viewing it from above, were two or three small cabins — inhabited, probably, by dependents of the seigneur.

I must have crouched for nearly an hour at the tunnel entrance, staring in stupefied wonder — for it grew dark, and one by one lights began to flare at the windows until the whole north wing and central portion of the building were illuminated. But the south wing, nearest me, was dark, and I surmised that this portion was not occupied.

Fortune still seemed to favour me, and with this conclusion and the thought of Jacqueline, I gained courage to advance again. It was almost dark now and growing bitterly cold. I felt in my pocket for my pistol and loaded it with the two cartridges that alone remained of the lot I had brought with me. Then I advanced stealthily until I stood beneath the cataract; and here I found the spray no longer drenched me. The splendid torrent shot out like a crystal arch above me — so strong and compact that only those at some distance could feel the mist that veiled it like a luminous garment.

I came upon a door in the dark wing and, turning the handle noiselessly, found myself inside the *château*. And at once my ears were filled with yells and coarse laughter of men's and women's voices. There was no storm door, and the interior of the *château* — at least, the wing in which I found myself — was almost as cold as the outside. I stood still, hesitating which way to take. A fiddle was being played somewhere, and the bursts of noisy laughter sounded at intervals.

As my eyes became accustomed to my surroundings, I perceived that I was standing near the foot of an uncarpeted wooden stairway. There was a dark room with an open door immediately in front of me, and another at the farther end of the passage, from beneath which a glimmer of light issued, and it was from this room that the sounds of laughter and music came.

While I was pondering upon my next movement, heavy footsteps fell on the storey above me, and a man began coming down the stairs. I stole into the dark room in front of me, and had hardly ensconced myself there than he brushed past and went into the room at the end of the hallway.

And I was certain that he was Leroux.

It was evident that he had not closed the door behind him, for the sounds of the fiddle and of the revelers became much more distinct. I had left my snowshoes near the entrance to the tunnel, and my moccasins made no sound upon the floor.

I crept out of my hiding place and went toward the open door. As I had surmised, this was the place of the assemblage. I crouched there, with my pistol in my hand. On the opposite side of the room

Simon Leroux was standing, a sneering smile upon his face.

The scene I saw through the crack of the door quite took my breath away. The room was an enormous one, evidently forming the entire central portion of the *château*. It was a ballroom, or had been a ballroom, once, for it had a wide hardwood floor, somewhat worn and uneven. The walls were hung with portraits, evidently of the owner's ancestors, for I caught a glimpse of several faces in wigs and periwigs.

The furniture was of an old type. Pushed against one wall, near where Leroux stood, was an ancient piano, and standing upon the other side an old man played upon a violin. He must have been nearly eighty years of age. His face had fallen in over the toothless gums, leaving the prominent cheek-bones protruding like those of a skull, and his head was a heavy mat of straight grey hair. He looked like a full-blooded Indian.

Two couples were dancing on the floor. Each man had an Indian woman. One was middle-aged; the other, a comely young woman with heavy silver earrings, was laughing noisily as her companion dragged her to a standstill in front of the fiddler.

'Play faster, Pierre Caribou!' he yelled, pushing the old man backward.

It was the man with the patch! 'Be quiet, Jean Petitjean,' exclaimed the woman, giving him a mock blow. 'Do not hurt my father!'

They laughed drunkenly and resumed the dance. The man with the older woman was not — greatly to my surprise — Jean Petitjean's companion of the night. The woman was addressing him as Raoul. She seemed trying to quiet him, for he was shouting boisterously as he twirled. From his post across the room, Leroux watched the proceedings with his sneering smile.

Flaring candles were set in sconces of wrought iron around the room, casting a pallid light upon the scene, and so unreal it would have been but for my recognition of the men that I might have expected it to disappear before my eyes. I crept back from the door and, tracing my journey along the corridor, began to ascend the stairs.

On the first storey I perceived a number of rooms, but those whose doors were open were dark and apparently empty. I imagined that all the magnificence of the *château* was concentrated in that big ballroom.

The corridor on the first storey had smaller passages opening out of it, one at each end. I turned to the left. Now the sound of the cataracts, which had never left my ears, became a din. The passages were full of stale tobacco smoke. And advancing, I suddenly found myself face to face with Philippe Lacroix.

He was seated at a table in a room writing, and I came right upon the door before I was aware of it. I saw his thin face with the little upturned moustache and the cold sneer about the mouth; and I think I should have shot him if he had looked up. But he neither heard nor saw me, but wrote steadily, puffing at a vile cigar, and I crept back from the door.

Thank God Jacqueline was not among those brutes below! But I shuddered to think of her environment here. I turned back and followed the corridor to the right, and came to a little hall toward the rear of the building, as I judged, where the noise of the torrents was less loud, although I now perceived that the *château* was in a continual mild tremor from the force of their discharge.

The windows in this little hall were broken in several places, and had evidently been in this condition for a long time, for they were covered with strips of paper, through which the wind entered in chilling gusts. Beyond me was an open door, and behind it I saw the dull glow of a stove and felt its heat. I approached cautiously and looked in.

I never saw a room so littered and uncared for. There were books around the walls and books upon the floor, covered with dust; there was dust and dirt and debris everywhere, and spider-webs along the walls and ceiling. The impression of the whole place was that of ruin. Facing me, above a cracked and ancient mirror, were two rusty broadswords, and in the mirror I saw a large oaken table reflected.

Seated at it, clothed in a threadbare coat of very ancient fashion, was an old man with long snow-white hair and a white forked beard. He was busily transferring a stack of gold pieces from his right to his left side; and then he began scribbling on a sheet of paper. He paid me not the smallest attention as I entered.

Not even when I stood beside him did he look up, but went on sorting out his coins and jotting down figures upon the paper. Sheets of it, covered with penciled figures, stood everywhere stacked upon the table, and other sheets were strewn among the books upon the floor; and while I watched, the old man laid aside the sheet he had been writing on and drew another sheet from the top of a thick pile beside him.

There was a door behind his chair, leading, I imagined, into a lumber room. I walked around the room and looked through it, but the place beyond was dark. Then I came back to the old man, who still paid me not the least attention.

Now I perceived that the top of the table was very curiously designed. It was marked off with squares and columns, and in each square were figures in black and red. Upon one end of the table at which the old man sat was a cup-shaped circular affair of very dark wood-teak, it resembled — once delicately inlaid with pearl. But now most of the inlay had disappeared, leaving unsightly holes. At the bottom of the cup were a number of metallic compartments, and the whole interior portion was revolving slowly at a turn of the old man's fingers. He picked a tiny ivory ball from the table and placed it in the cup. He set the interior spinning and the ball circulating in the reverse direction. The sphere clicked and clattered as it forced its way among the metallic strips.

It may seem strange that I did not at first recognize a roulette-wheel. But the game is more a diversion of the rich than of those with whom fortune had thrown me. Gambling had never appealed to me, and I knew roulette only by reputation.

The ball stopped and settled in one of the compartments, and the old man took a gold piece from one of the squares on the table, transferred a little pile of gold from his right side to his left, and jotted down some figures upon his paper.

And suddenly I was aware of an abysmal rage that filled me. It seemed like an abominable dream — the futile old man, the ruffians and their wenches below. And I had endured so much for Jacqueline, to find myself enmeshed in such things in the end. I stepped forward and swept the entire heap of gold into the centre of the table.

'M. Duchaine!' I shouted. 'Why are you playing the fool here when your daughter is suffering persecution?'

The old man seemed to be aware of my presence for the first time. He looked up at me out of his mild old eyes, and shook his head in apparent perplexity.

'You are welcome, *monsieur*,' he said, half-rising with a courtly air. 'Do you wish to stake a few pieces in a game with me?' He gathered up a handful of the coins and pushed them toward me. 'Of course, we shall give back our stakes at the end,' he continued, eyeing me with a cunning expression in which I seemed to detect avarice and madness, too. 'This is just to see how well we play. Afterward, if we are satisfied, we will play for real money — real gold.'

He began to divide the gold pieces into two heaps.

'You see, *monsieur*, I have a system — at least, I nearly have a system,' he went on eagerly. 'But it may not be so good as yours. Come. You shall be the banker, and see if you can win my money from me. But we shall return the stakes afterward.'

'M. Duchaine!' I shouted in his ear. 'Where is your daughter?'

'My daughter,' he repeated in mild surprise. 'Ah, yes; she has gone to New York to make our fortune with the system. You see,' he continued with senile cunning, 'she has taken away the system, and so I am not sure whether I can beat you. But make your play, *monsieur*.'

There was at least no indecision in the manner in which he set the wheel spinning. I did not know what to do. I was fascinated and bewildered by the situation. In desperation, I thrust a gold piece upon one of the numbers at the head of a column. The wheel stopped, and the ball rolled into one of its compartments. The old man thrust several gold pieces toward me.

I staked again and again, and won every time. Within five minutes, the whole heap of gold pieces lay at my side. The dotard looked at me with an expression of imbecile terror.

'You will give them back to me?' he pleaded. 'Remember, *monsieur*, it was agreed that we should return the money.'

I thrust the heap of coins toward him. 'Now, M. Duchaine,' I said, 'in return for these you will conduct me to Mlle. Jacqueline.' He shook his head as though he had not understood.

'It is very strange,' he said. 'I do not understand it at all. The system cannot be at fault; and yet — '

I snatched the paper from his grasp and threw it on the floor, then pulled him to his feet. 'Enough of this nonsense, M. Duchaine,' I said. 'Will you conduct me to Mlle. Jacqueline immediately, or shall I go and find her?'

'I am here, *monsieur*,' answered a voice at the door; and I whirled, to see Jacqueline confronting me.

14

Some Plain Speaking

I took three steps toward her and stood still. For this was Jacqueline; but it was not *my* Jacqueline. It might have been Jacqueline's grandmother when she was a woman — this haughty belle with her high waist and side curls, and her flounced skirt and aspect of cold recognition.

She did not stir as I approached her, but stood still, framed in the doorway, looking at me as though I were an unwelcome stranger. My outstretched arms fell to my sides. I halted three paces in front of her. There was no answering welcome on her face, only a cold little smile that showed she knew me.

'Jacqueline!' I cried. 'It's me, Paul! You know me, Jacqueline?'

Jacqueline inclined her head. 'Oh, yes; I know you, *monsieur*,' she answered. 'Why have you come here?'

'To see you, Jacqueline! To save you!'

She made me a mocking courtesy. 'I am infinitely obliged to you, *monsieur*, for your goodwill,' she said, 'but I do not need your aid. I am with friends now, M. Paul!'

I withdrew a little way and leaned my hand against the table for support, breathing heavily. Behind me I heard the click, click of the roulette ball as it pursued its course around the wheel. The old dotard had already forgotten me, and was playing with his right hand against his left again.

'Do you not want to see me, Jacqueline?' I asked, watching her through a whirling fog.

'No, *monsieur*,' she answered chillingly.

'Do you wish me to go?'

She said nothing, and I walked unsteadily toward the door. She followed me slowly. I went out of the room and pulled the door to behind me.

She opened it and stood confronting me; and then burst into a flood of impassioned speech. 'Why have you followed me here to persecute me?' she cried. 'Are you under the illusion that I am helpless? Do you think the friends who rescued me from you have forgotten that you exist? You took advantage of my helplessness. I do not want to see you. I hate you!'

'You told me that you loved me, and I believed you, Jacqueline,' I answered miserably, watching the colour flame to her lovely face. And I could see she remembered that.

'When I was ill you used me for your own base schemes,' she went on with cutting emphasis. 'And you — you followed me here. Do you think that I am unprotected, and that you are dealing only with an old man and a helpless woman? Why, I have friends who would come in and kill you if I but raised my voice!'

'Raise your voice, *mademoiselle*. I am ready for your friends,' I answered.

She looked less steadily at me and seemed to waver. 'What have you come for?' she asked. 'Have you not had money enough? Do you want more?'

I seized her by the wrists. Thus I held

her at arm's length, and my fingers tightened until I saw the flesh grow white beneath them. The intensity of my rage beat hers down and made it a puny thing.

'Jacqueline! You take me for an adventurer?' I cried. 'Is that what they told you? Why do you think I brought you so near your home when you were, as you said, helpless? Only a few nights ago you said you loved me; that you would never send me away until I wished to go. What is it that has happened to change you so, Jacqueline?' I had her in my arms.

She struggled fiercely, and I let her go. 'How dare you, *monsieur*!' she panted. 'Go at once, or I shall call for aid!'

So I went into the passage; and as I left the room I could still hear the hellish click of the ivory ball in the roulette-wheel. I was utterly confounded. But before I reached the end of the little hall, Jacqueline came running back to me.

'*Monsieur*!' she gasped. 'M. Paul! For the sake of — of what I once thought you, I do not want you to be seen. You are in dreadful danger. Come back!'

'Never mind the danger, *madame*,' I

answered, and I saw her flinch at the word and look at me in dazed bewilderment. 'Never mind *my* danger.'

'It is for your own sake, *monsieur*,' she said more gently.

'No, Mme. d'Epernay,' I answered; and she winced again, as though I had struck her across the face.

'For my sake,' she pleaded, catching at my arm, and at that moment I heard a door slam underneath and heavy footsteps begin slowly to ascend the stairs.

'No, *madame*,' I answered, trying to release my arm from her clasp. Her face was full of fear, and I knew it was fear of the man below, not me.

'Then for the sake of — our love, Paul!' she gasped.

I suffered her to lead me back into the room. As she drew me back and closed the door behind us, I heard the footsteps pause and turn along the corridor. I knew that heavy gait as well as though I already saw Leroux's hard face before my eyes.

Jacqueline pushed me inside the room behind her father's chair and closed, but did not hasp, the door. The room was completely dark, and I did not know whether it connected with other rooms or was a mere closet, but the freshness of the air in it inclined me to the former view.

Over my head the torrent roared, and I had to stand very close to the door to hear what passed. I heard Leroux tramp in and his voice mingling with the *click-click* of the ball in the roulette-wheel.

'Who is here?' he demanded.

'I am,' answered Jacqueline.

'I thought I heard Lacroix,' said Leroux thickly.

'I have not seen M. Lacroix today,' Jacqueline returned.

Leroux stamped heavily about the room and then sat down. I heard the legs of his chair scratch the wooden floor as he drew it up to the table.

'*Maudit!*' he burst out explosively. 'Where is d'Epernay? I am tired of waiting for him!'

'I have told you many times that I do not know,' answered Jacqueline; and there followed the *click-click* of the ball inside the wheel again.

'How long will you keep up this pretence, *madame*?' cried Leroux angrily. 'What have you to gain by concealing the knowledge of your husband from me?'

'M. Leroux, why will you not believe that I remember nothing?' answered Jacqueline.

'How can you have forgotten? Why did you run away after marrying him? What were you doing in New York? Who was the man who accompanied you to the Merrimac?' he shouted.

Through the chink of the door I saw the old man look up in mild protest at the disturbing sounds. I clenched my fists, and the temptation to make an end of Leroux was almost too strong for my restraint. But to Jacqueline the insult conveyed no meaning, and Leroux continued in more moderate tones.

'Come, *madame*, why do you not play fair with me?' he asked. 'Who is that man Hewlett, and why did he accompany you so far toward your *chateau*? Before God, I know your husband and he have been plotting with Tom Carson against me, but why he should thus place himself in my power I cannot understand.'

'Ah, you have spoken of a Tom Carson many times,' said Jacqueline. 'Soon, *monsieur*, I shall begin to believe that such a person really exists.'

'Tell me where you met Hewlett.'

'I tell you for the last time, *monsieur*, that I do not remember. But what I do remember I shall tell you. After my father had turned M. Louis d'Epernay out of his home, whither he had come to beg money to pay his gambling debts, you brought him back. You made my father take him in. He wanted to marry me. But I refused, because I had no love for him. But you insisted I should marry him, because he had gained you the entrance to the seigniory and helped you to acquire your power over my father. Oh, yes, *monsieur*, let us be frank with each other, as you have expressed the desire to be.'

'Go on,' growled Leroux, biting his lip. 'Perhaps I shall learn something.'

'Nothing that you do not already know, *monsieur*,' she flashed out with spirit. 'My father came here, long ago, a political fugitive, in danger of death. You knew this, and you played upon his fears. You brought your friends and encouraged him to gamble and waste his money in his old age, when his mind had become enfeebled.

'Yes, you played on the old gambling instinct which had laid dormant in him for forty years. You made him think he was acting the grand seigneur, as his father had done in earlier days, in his other home at St. Boniface. You drained him of his last penny, and then you offered him ten thousand dollars to gamble with in Quebec, telling him of the delights of the city and promising him immunity,' the woman went on remorselessly. 'And for this he was to assign his property to Louis, thinking, of course, that he could soon make his fortune at the tables. And Louis was to marry me, and in turn sell the seigniory to you. And so I married Louis under threat of death to my father. Oh, yes, *monsieur*, the plan was simple and well devised. And I knew nothing of it. But Louis d'Epernay blurted it all out to me upon our wedding night. I think the shame of knowing that I had been sold to him unhinged my mind, for I ran out into the snows. Now you know all, *monsieur*, for I remember nothing more until I found myself travelling back with M. Hewlett in the sleigh. You say I was in New York. Well, I do not remember it. And as for Louis d'Epernay, I know *nothing* of him — but I will *die* before he claims me as his *wife!*'

She had grown breathless as she proceeded with her scathing denunciation, and now stood facing him with an aspect of fearless challenge on her face. And then I had the measure of Leroux. He laughed, and he beat down her scorn with scorn.

'You have underestimated your price, *madame*,' he sneered. 'Since you have learned so much, I will tell you more. You have cost me twenty thousand dollars, and not ten; for besides the ten thousand paid to your father, Louis got ten thousand also, upon the signing of the marriage contract. So swallow that, and be proud of being priced so high! And the seigniory is already his, and I am waiting for him to return and sell me the ground rights for twenty-five thousand more, and if I know Louis d'Epernay he will not wait very long to get his fingers on it.'

Jacqueline stood watching him with supreme indifference. The man's coarse gibes had flown past her without wounding her, as they would have hurt a lower nature. 'No doubt he will return,' she answered quietly. 'If he would take ten thousand for me, surely he will take twenty-five thousand for the seigniory. You have us in your power.'

'Then why the devil doesn't he come?' roared Leroux. 'If he is intriguing with Carson, by God, I know enough to shut him up in jail the rest of his life. And so, *madame*,' he ended quietly, 'it will perhaps be worth your while to tell me why Tom Carson sent this Hewlett back to the *château*; for no doubt the wolves have picked him pretty clean by now.'

'Listen to me, Simon Leroux,' said Jacqueline, standing up before him, as indomitable in spirit as he. 'All your plots and schemes mean nothing to me. My only aim is to take my father away from here, from you and M. d'Epernay, and let you wrangle over your spoil. There are more than four-legged wolves, M. Leroux; there are human ones, and, like the others, when food is scarce they prey upon each other.'

'I like your spirit!' exclaimed Simon, staring at her with frank admiration.

And Jacqueline's head drooped then. Unwittingly, Simon had pierced her defences. But he never knew, for before he had time to know, the greybeard rose upon his feet and rubbed his thin hands together, chuckling.

'Never mind your money, Simon,' he said. 'I'm going to be richer than any of you. Do you know what I did with that ten thousand? I gave it to my little daughter, and she has gone to New York to make our fortunes at Mr. Daly's gaming-house. No, there she is!' he suddenly exclaimed. 'She has come back!'

Leroux wheeled round and looked from one to the other. 'So that was the purpose of your visit to New York?' he asked Jacqueline. 'So — you have not quite forgotten that, *madame*! Your price was not too vile a thing for you to take it to New York with you! Your shame was not too great for you to remember that your father had ten thousand dollars!'

'It was not mine,' she flashed back at Leroux. 'My father would have lost it again to you. I took it to New York because I thought that I could make enough to give him a home during the rest of his days. Do you think I would have touched a penny of it, *monsieur*?'

'I don't know,' answered Leroux. 'But we will soon find out. Where is that money, *madame*?'

Jacqueline's lips quivered. I saw her glance involuntarily toward the door behind which I was standing. And suddenly the last phase of the problem became clear to me. Jacqueline thought I had robbed her. I stepped from behind the door and faced Leroux.

'I have that money,' I said curtly.

I saw his face turn white. He staggered back, and then, with a bull's bellow, rushed at me, his heavy fists aloft. I think he could have beaten out my brains with them. But he stopped short when he saw my automatic pistol pointing at his chest. And he saw in my face that I was ready to shoot to kill.

'You thief — you spy — you treacher-
ous hound, I'll murder you!' he roared.

The dotard, who had been looking at
me, came forward. 'No, no, I won't have
him murdered, Simon,' he protested,
laying a trembling hand on Leroux's
shoulder. 'He has almost as good a
roulette system as I have.'

15

Won-and-Lost

We must have stood confronting each other for fully a minute. Then Leroux dropped his hands and smiled sourly at me.

'You seem — temporarily — to have the advantage of me, M. Hewlett,' he said. 'I respect your pertinacity, and now at last I am content in having discovered the motive of your enterprise. I thought you were hired by Carson. If you had been frank with me, we might have come to an understanding long ago. So, since you have managed to come thus far, and since I am a man of business, the best thing we can do is to talk over our difficulties and try to adjust them. You will recall that on the occasion of our meeting in New York, I asked you what your price was. But of course you were not then prepared to answer me, since you had your price already. Well, have you come here to get more?'

There was an indescribable insolence in his tone. In spite of the fact that I had him at my mercy, the man's force and courage almost made him my master then. 'You may leave us, Mme. d'Epernay,' he said to Jacqueline. 'No doubt your absence will spare your feelings, for we are going to be frank in our speech.'

'I thank you for your consideration, M. Leroux,' replied Jacqueline, and walked quietly out of the room. It occurred to me that Leroux could hardly be more frank than he had been, but I sat down and waited. The ball was clicking round the wheel again, and very faintly, through the roar of the cataracts, I heard the sound of the fiddle below.

Leroux sat down heavily. 'I will put down my cards,' he said. 'I have you here in my power. I have four men with me. This dotard' — he glanced contemptuously at old Duchaine — 'has no bearing on the situation. You can, of course, kill me; but that would not help you. You are in possession of some money belonging to

Mme. d'Epernay, and also of certain information that I shall be glad to receive. There is no law in this valley except my will. Give me the information I want, keep your money, and go.'

I waited.

'In the first place, are you or are you not in Carson's pay? I shall believe your answer, because if you are, I shall offer you a better price to join me, and therefore it will not pay you to lie. But you will not be able to deceive me by pretending to be.'

'I am not,' I answered.

'Then why did he send you here?'

'I left his employ three days before I met Mme. d'Epernay. If you were in New York, you must have seen that I was not there.'

'Good. Second, where is Louis d'Epernay?'

'I have never seen the man,' I replied.

Leroux glanced incredulously at me. 'Then your meeting with *madame* was purely an accident?' he inquired. 'Your only desire, then, was to get the money you knew she was carrying with her? But how did you know that she was carrying that money?'

I shrugged my shoulders. How was it possible for us to reach an understanding?

'I don't know why you are lying to me,' he said. 'It is not to your advantage. You must have known that she was in New York; Louis must have told Carson, and he must have told you. And Louis must have told you the secret of the entrance, unless — '

'Listen to me!' I snapped. 'I will not be badgered with any more questions. I have told you the truth. I met Mme. d'Epernay by accident, and I escorted her toward the *chateau*, and followed her after you kidnapped her, to protect her from you.'

He grunted and glanced at me with an inscrutable expression upon his hard features. 'You are in love with her?' he asked.

'Put it that way if you choose,' I answered.

He scowled at me ferociously, and then he began studying my face. I returned stare for stare. Finally he banged his big fist down upon the table.

'Well, it doesn't matter,' he said, 'because, whatever your purpose, you cannot do any harm. And you understand that she is a married woman. So you will, no doubt, agree to take your money and depart?'

'I shall go if she tells me to go,' I answered; but even while I spoke my heart sank, for I had little hope.

'That is easily settled,' answered Leroux. 'I will bring her back and you shall hear the decision from her own lips.'

He left the room, and I sat there alone beside the dotard, listening to the click of the ball and the chink of the coins, and the roar of the twin cataracts above. In truth, I had no further excuse for staying. I knew what Jacqueline's reply must be. But there had been a sinister smoothness in Leroux's latest mood. I did not trust the man, for all his bluntness. I suspected something, and I did not intend to relax my guard.

A gentle touch upon the elbow made me leap round in my chair. Old Charles Duchaine had ceased to play and was watching me out of his mild eyes. His fingers stroked my coat sleeve timidly, as though he were afraid of me.

'Don't go away!' he said with a shrewd leer. 'Don't go away!'

'Eh?' I exclaimed, startled at this answer to my own self-questioning.

'Simon is a bad man,' whispered the greybeard, putting his nodding head close down to mine. 'He won't let you go away. He never lets *anyone* go when they have come here. He didn't know my little daughter was going, but I was too clever for him, because he wasn't here. They think I am a silly old man, but I know more than they think. Simon thinks he has got me in his power, but he hasn't.'

'How is that?' I inquired, startled at the man's sincerity. I fancied that he must have been pretending to be half-imbecile for reasons of his own.

'I have a system,' leered the dotard. 'I can win thousands and millions with it. I have been perfecting it for years. I have sent my little daughter to New York to play. Then I shall put Simon out of the house and we shall all be happy in Quebec together.'

I turned from him in disgust, and, after ineffectually tapping my arm for a few moments, he went back to his wheel. But, though I was disappointed to discover that my surmise as to his playing a part was incorrect, his words set me thinking. An imbecile old person is often a fair reader of character. Was Simon plotting something?

He came back with Jacqueline before I could decide. 'If you bid him, *madame*, M. Hewlett is willing to take his departure,' said Leroux to her. 'Is it your wish that he remain or go?'

'Oh, I want you to go, *monsieur*,' said Jacqueline, clasping her hands pleadingly. Her eyes were full of tears, which trickled down her cheeks, and she turned her head away. 'There is no reason why you should remain, *monsieur*,' she said.

'Are you saying this of your free will, Jacqueline?' I cried.

She nodded, and I saw Simon's evil face crease with suppressed mirth.

I rose up. 'Adieu, then, *madame*,' I said. 'But first permit me to restore the money that I have been keeping for you.' And I took out my pocketbook.

Simon stared at me incredulously. 'I do

not understand you in the least, now, M. Hewlett,' he exclaimed. 'You are to keep the money. I do not go back upon my bargains.'

'It is not, however, your money,' I retorted, though I knew that it soon would be. 'I shall return it to Mme. d'Epernay, who entrusted me with it. Beyond that, I care nothing as to its ultimate destination, though perhaps I can guess. Naturally I do not carry eight thousand dollars about with me — '

'Ten thousand!' shouted Simon.

'Mme. d'Epernay gave me eight thousand,' I said. 'I do not know anything about ten thousand. Probably Mr. Daly has the rest. But, as I was saying, I shall give you a cheque — '

Leroux burst into loud laughter and slapped me heartily upon the shoulder.

'Paul Hewlett,' he said, with genuine admiration, 'you are as good as a play. My friend, it would have paid you to have accepted my own offer. However, you declined it and I shall not renew it. Well, let us take your cheque, and it shall be accepted in full settlement.' He winked at me and thrust his tongue into his cheek.

I was too sick at heart to pay attention to his buffoonery. I sat down at the table and, taking up a pen which lay there, wrote a check for eight thousand dollars, making it out to Jacqueline d'Epernay. This I handed to her.

'Adieu, *madame*,' I said.

'Adieu, *monsieur*,' she answered almost inaudibly, her head bent low.

I went out of the room, still gripping my pistol, and I took care to let Simon see it as we descended the stairs side by side. The noisy laughter in the ballroom had ceased, but I heard Raoul and Jean Petitjean quarrelling, and their thick voices told me that they were in no condition to aid their master. Then there were only Leroux and Philippe Lacroix to deal with. I could have saved the situation. What a fool I had been! What an irresolute fool! I never learned.

As we reached the bottom of the stairs, Philippe Lacroix came out of the ballroom carrying a candle. I saw his melancholy, pale face twist with surprise as he perceived me.

'Philippe, this is M. Paul Hewlett,' said Leroux. 'Tomorrow you will convey him to the cabin of Père Antoine, where he will be able to make his own plans. You will go by way of *le Vieil Ange*.'

Lacroix started violently, muttered something, and passed up the stairs, often turning to stare, as I surmised from the brief occasions of his footsteps.

'Now, M. Hewlett, I shall show you your sleeping quarters for tonight,' Leroux continued to me, and conducted me out into the fenced yard. A number of huskies were lying there, and one of them came bounding up to me and began to sniff at my clothes, betraying every sign of recognition.

This I knew to be the beast that I had taken to the home. How it had managed to make its escape, I could not imagine; but it had evidently come northward with hardly a pause; and not only that, but had accompanied us on our journey from St. Boniface at a distance, like the half-wild creature that it was.

Two sleighs were standing before the huts. Leroux led me past them and knocked at the door of the largest cabin. 'Pierre Caribou!' he shouted.

He was facing the door and did not see what I saw at the little window on the other side. I saw the face of the old Indian, distorted with a grimace of fury as he eyed Leroux. Next moment he stood cringing before him, his features a mask. Looking in, I saw a huge stove which nearly filled the interior, and seated beside it the middle-aged squaw.

'This gentleman will sleep here tonight,' said Leroux curtly. 'In the morning at sunrise, harness a sleigh for him and M. Lacroix. Adieu, M. Hewlett,' he continued, turning to me. 'And be sure your check will never be presented.'

There was something so sinister in his manner that again I felt that thrill of fear which he seemed able to inspire in me. He was less human than any man I had known. He impressed me always as the incarnation of resolute evil. He swung upon his heel and left me.

I went in with Pierre Caribou, and the squaw glided out of the cabin. There were two couches of the kind they used to call ottomans inside, which had evidently once formed part of the *château* furnishings for their faded splendour accorded little with the decrepit interior of the hut.

I looked at my watch. I had thought it must be midnight, and it was only eight. Within three hours, I had won Jacqueline and lost her forever. With Leroux in my power, I had yielded and gone away.

And on the morrow, I should arrive at Père Antoine's hut just when he expected me. Surely the mockery of fate could go no further!

I sank down on one of the divans and buried my face in my hands, while Pierre Caribou busied himself preparing food over the stove.

16

The Old Angel

Presently the Indian touched me on the shoulder, and I looked up. He had a plateful of steaming stew in his hands, and set it down beside me. 'Eat!' he said in English.

I was too dispirited and dejected to obey him at first. But soon I managed to fall to, and I was surprised to discover how ravenous I was. I had eaten hardly anything for days, and only a few mouthfuls since morning.

As I was eating, there came a scratching at the door, and the husky pushed its way into the cabin and came bounding to my side. I stroked and petted it, and gave it the remnants of my meal, while Pierre watched us.

'You know this dog?' he asked,

'I saw it in New York,' I answered. 'It brought me to Mlle. Jacqueline.'

My mind was very much alert just then. It was as though some hidden monitor within me had taken control to guide me through a maze of unknown dangers. It was that inner prompting which had forbidden me to say, 'Mme. d'Epernay.'

I had a consciousness of some impending horror. And I was shaking and all a sweat — with fear, too — gripping fear! Yet the old name sounded as sweet as ever to my lips. The Indian drew the stool near me and sat down.

'You met Mlle. Jacqueline in New York?' he asked.

'I brought her back,' I answered.

'I know,' the Indian answered. 'I met Simon; drove him from St. Boniface to the *château*. He wanted to shoot you. I said no; you were snow-blind, so he should leave you to die there. I took Ma'm'selle Jacqueline to St. Boniface, when she ran way. Simon was not here then or I would have been afraid. Simon is a bad man. He gave my woman to Jean Petitjean. My woman was a good woman till Simon give her to that bad man. I will kill him one day.'

I saw a glimmer of hope now, though of what I hardly knew; or perhaps it was only the desire to talk of Jacqueline and hear her name upon my lips and Pierre's. 'Pierre Caribou,' I said, 'wouldn't you like to have the old days back when M. Duchaine was master and there was no Simon Leroux?'

He did not answer me, but I saw his face muscles twitch. Then he pulled a pipe from his pocket and stuffed it with a handful of coarse tobacco. He handed it to me and struck a match and held it to the bowl. When the tobacco was alight, he took another pipe and began smoking also. I had not smoked for days, and I inhaled the rank tobacco fumes through the old pipe gratefully. I was smoking with an Indian, and that meant what it has always meant. A black cloud seemed to have been lifted from my mind. And I was not trembling anymore. But how warily I was reaching out toward my companion.

'Pierre, I came here to save Mlle. Jacqueline,' I said.

'No can save her,' he answered. 'No can

fight against Simon.'

'What in the devil's name, is his power, then?' I cried.

'*Le diable*,' he replied. He may have misunderstood me, but the answer was apt. 'No use fighting him,' he said. 'All in the past now. Perhaps old Pierre will kill him; nobody else.' He looked steadily at me. 'I poisoned his dogs,' he added.

'What?' I exclaimed.

'Simon told me long ago nobody comes to the *château*. What did he tell you — are you going?'

'Lacroix is going to take me to Père Antoine's cabin tomorrow morning,' I answered.

The Indian grunted. 'Simon doesn't mean to let you go,' he said. 'He means to kill you. You know too much. Sometime he'll kill me, too, or I'll kill him. Once I lived in the old *château* at St. Boniface with old M'sieur Duchaine. Good days then, not like now. Hunted plenty of game. Fine people come from Quebec, not like Simon. M'sieur Charles was a small boy then. All in the past now.'

'Pierre,' I said, taking him by the arm,

'what is the Old Angel — *le Vieil Ange*?'

He stared stolidly at me. 'Why do you ask?' he said.

'Because Lacroix has been instructed to take me by that route.'

Pierre said not a word, but smoked in silence. I sat upon the couch waiting. His face was quite impassive, but I knew that my question was of tremendous import to me. At last he shook the ashes out of his pipe and rose.

'Come with me,' he said. 'I'll show you — because you're a friend of Ma'm'selle Jacqueline. Come.'

I followed him out of the hut. A large moon was just rising out of the east, but it was not yet high enough to cast much light.

Still Pierre seemed in deadly terror of Simon, for he motioned me to creep, as he was creeping, out of the enclosure, bending low beside the fence, so that a watcher from the *château* might not detect our silhouettes against the snow-covered lake. When we were clear of the *château*, or, rather, the lit portion of it, Pierre began to run swiftly, still in a crouching position, and in this way we gained the tunnel entrance.

He took me by the arm, for it was too dark for me to follow him by sight, and we traversed perhaps a mile of outer blackness. Then I began to see a gleam of moonlight in front of me, and, though I had not been conscious of making any turn, I discovered that we must have retraced our course completely, for I heard the roar of the cataracts again.

Then we emerged upon a tiny shelf of rock some forty feet up the face of the wall, and quite invisible from below. It was a little above the level of the *château* roof, about a hundred yards away. Below me I could see the main entrance to the tunnel. We had a foothold of about ten feet on the level platform, which was slippery with smooth black ice; and thundering over us, so near that I could almost have touched it had I stretched out my hand, the whirling torrent plunged into that hell below. It was a terrific scene. Above us, that stream of white water, resembling nothing so much as a high-pressure jet from a fireman's hose magnified a thousand times, curved like a crystal arch, and so compact by reason of its force that not a drop splashed us. It was as strong as a steel girder, and I think it would have cut steel.

Pierre caught my arm as I reeled, sick with the shock of the discovery, and yelled into my ear above the dim. '*Le Vieil Ange!*' he cried. 'This is the way Simon meant you to go tomorrow. Lacroix would tell you: 'Get down, we'll find the road.' He would take you up here and push you — so.' He made a graphic gesture with his arm and pointed.

I looked down, shuddering, into the black foam-crested water, bubbling and whirling among the grotesque ice pillars that stood like sentries upon the brink. The horror of the plot quite unmanned me. I groped for the shelter of the tunnel, and clung to the rocky wall to save myself from obeying a wild impulse to cast myself headlong into the flood below. I perceived now that the whole face of the wall was honeycombed with tunnels of natural formation running into the recesses of the limestone. I wondered that the whole structure, undermined thus and pressed down by the weight of millions of tons of ice above where the glacier lay, did not collapse and crumble down in ruin. Rivulets gushed from the wall everywhere, mingling their contributory waters with those of the twin torrents. The plateau seemed to be the watershed in which the drainage of the entire territory had its origin. Within those connecting caves, if a man knew their secret, he might hide from a regiment.

Pierre followed me to the mouth of the tunnel and gripped me by both arms. 'What will you do?' he asked. 'Will you go to Père Antoine tonight? What will you do now?'

I took the pistol from my coat pocket. 'Pierre,' I answered, 'I have two bullets here, and both of them are for Simon. Tonight I had him in my power and spared him. Now I am going back, and I shall shoot him down like a dog, whether he is armed or defenceless.'

'*Le diable* is his friend. You had him tonight; why did you not shoot him then?'

I did not know. But I was going to find out soon. 'I am going back to kill him now,' I repeated. 'Afterward I do not know what will happen. But you can go on to the hut of Père Antoine and, if luck is with me, I shall meet you there — perhaps with Mlle. Jacqueline.' But I had little hope of meeting him with Jacqueline. Only I could not forbear to speak her name again.

Pierre's face was twitching. 'You must not go back!' he cried. 'Simon will kill you. No use fighting Simon. His time has not come yet. When his time comes, he will die.'

'When will it come?' I asked, looking at the man's features, which were distorted with frenzied hate.

'I do not know!' exclaimed Pierre. 'I try to find — cards to tell me. No Indian man in this part country remembers how to tell me. In the old days, many could tell. Now I wait. When his time comes, I will know. I will kill Simon then myself. Nobody else must kill Simon. No use for you to try.'

I own that, standing there and thinking

upon the man's hellish design, his unscrupulousness, his singular success, I felt the old fear of Leroux in my heart, and with it something of the same superstition of his invulnerability. But my resolution surpassed my fear, and I knew it would not fail me. I shook the Indian's hands away and plunged forward into the tunnel again. I heard him calling after me; but I think he saw that I was not to be deterred, for he made no attempt to follow me. And so I went on through the darkness, and with each step toward the *château* my resolution grew.

I seemed to have been travelling for a much longer period than before. Every moment, straining my eyes, I expected to see the light of the entrance; but the road went on straight apparently, and there was nothing but the darkness.

At last I stood still; and then, just as I was thinking of retracing my steps, I felt a breath of air upon my forehead. I hurried on again, and in another minute I saw a faint light in front of me. Presently it grew more distinct. I was approaching the tunnel's mouth. But I stopped again. I was waiting for something — to *hear* something that I did not hear. Then I knew that it was the sound of the waterfalls. In place of them, there was only the gurgling of a brook.

My elbow grated against the tunnel wall. I stepped sidewise toward the centre, and ran against the wall opposite. Now, by the stronger light, I could see that I had strayed once again into some byway, for the passage was hardly three feet wide, and the low roof almost touched my head. It narrowed and grew lower still; but the light of the stars was clear in front of me and the cold wind blew upon my face; and I squeezed through into the same scooped-out hollow which I had entered on the same afternoon during the course of my journey toward the *château*.

I had approached it apparently through a mere fissure in the rocks upon the opposite side and at a point where I had assured myself that there could be no passage. The little river gurgled at my feet, and in front of me I saw a candle flickering in the recesses of a cave, so elfin that I could distinguish it only by shielding my eyes against the moon and stars.

I grasped my pistol tightly and crept noiselessly forward. If this should be Leroux, as I was convinced it was, I would not parley with him. I would shoot him down in his tracks.

My moccasined feet pressed the soft ground without the slightest sound. I gained the entrance to the cave. Within it, his back toward me, a man was stooping down. As I stepped nearer him, my feet dislodged a pebble, which rolled with a splash into the bed of the stream.

The man started and spun around, and I saw before me the pale, melancholy features of Philippe Lacroix.

17

Louis d'Epernay

He uttered an oath and took two steps backward, but I saw that he was unarmed and that he realized his helplessness. He flung his hands above his head and stood facing me, surprise and terror twisting his features into a grimacing grin. There was no man, next to Leroux, whom I would rather have seen.

'I wanted to see you, M. Hewlett,' he babbled.

'I can *quite* believe that, M. Lacroix,' I answered. 'You have looked for me before. But this time you have found me.'

'I have something of importance to say to you, *monsieur*,' he began again.

'I can believe that, too,' I answered. 'It is about *le Vieil Ange*, is it not?'

'By God, I did not mean — I swear to you, *monsieur* — listen, *monsieur*, one moment only,' he stammered. 'Lower your pistol. You see that I am unarmed!'

I lowered it. 'Well, say what you have to say,' I said to him.

'Leroux is a devil!' he burst out with no pretended passion. 'I want you to help me, M. Hewlett, and I can help you in a way you do not dream of. I am not one of his kind, to take his orders. Why, in Quebec, he would be like the dirt beneath my feet. He has a hold over me; he tempted me to gamble in one of his houses, and I — well, he has a hold over me. But he shall not drive me into murder. M. Hewlett, how much do you think this seigniory is worth?'

'I am not a financier,' I answered. 'Some half a million dollars, perhaps.'

He came close to me and hissed into my ear: '*Monsieur*, there is more gold in these rocks than anywhere in the world! Look here! Here!' He stooped down and began tossing pebbles at my feet. But they were pebbles of pure gold, and each one of them was as large as the first joint of my thumb. And I had misjudged his courage, I think, for it was avarice and not fear that made him tremble. So *that* was

Lacroix's master passion! I had always associated it with decrepit old age, as in the case of Charles Duchaine.

I looked into the cave. Lacroix was bending over a great heap of sacks, piled almost to the roof. They were sacks of earth, but the earth was flaked with gold, and I saw nuggets glittering in it.

'It is *everywhere, monsieur!*' cried Lacroix. 'In this stream, in these hills, too. You can gather a mortarful of earth anywhere, and it will show colour when it is washed. We found this place together — '

'You and Leroux?'

'No! I and — ' He broke off suddenly and eyed me with furtive cunning. 'Yes, yes, *monsieur*, Leroux and I. And we two worked here together, with nothing more than picks and shovels and mortars and pestles, Leroux and I. There was nobody else. We slept here when Duchaine thought we were in Quebec. For days and days we washed and dug, and we have hardly scratched the surface. *Monsieur*, it is the mother lode, it is the world's treasure house! There are millions upon millions here!'

I understood now why the provisions had been stored there. And I had passed by and never known that there was an ounce of gold! But — 'There are three blankets here,' I said.

'Yes, yes, *monsieur*!' cried Lacroix eagerly. 'I suffer much from cold. Two of them are mine, and Leroux has only one. It is the richest gold deposit in the world, M. Hewlett, and neither Raoul nor Jean Petitjean knows the secret — only Leroux and I. One cannot light upon this place save by a miracle of chance such as brought you here. God put this treasure in these hills, and He did not mean it to be found.'

I grasped him by the shoulder. 'Do you see what this means?' I shouted.

'It means a glorious life!' he cried. 'All the wealth in the world — '

'No, it means *death*!' I answered. 'It means that if Leroux succeeds in killing me, he will kill you, too! Don't you see that we must stand together? Do you suppose that he will share his hoard with you?'

'No, M. Hewlett,' answered Lacroix

quietly. 'And that is precisely what I wanted to say to you. You are not a hog like Leroux; I can trust you. And then you are a gentleman, and we gentlemen trust each other. I will give you a share of the gold, and you will get *mademoiselle*. She has no love for Louis. She left him half an hour after the marriage had been performed. Leroux witnessed the ceremony, and he hurried away with Père Antoine, and then she ran away. She loves you! And Louis will not trouble you!'

'*Faugh*!' I muttered. 'I don't want to hear your views on — on Mlle. Jacqueline, my friend. But it seems to me that our interests are mutual, and, as it happens, I was on my way back to have it out with Leroux when I stumbled upon this place.'

'But I can show you the way,' he exclaimed. 'Come with me, *monsieur*. I don't know how you got into the wrong passage, but it is straight ahead. Come with me! I will precede you.'

I followed him into the darkness, and very soon heard the sound of the cataract again. And then once more I was standing at the tunnel entrance, under a brilliant moon, and the *château* was before me.

It was all dark now, except for a glimmer of light that came from two windows on the far side, visible indirectly as a reflection from the snowy steeps beyond. That must be Duchaine's room.

Leroux's I did not know, of course, but I surmised that it was one of those on the same storey, which I had passed while making my previous tour of discovery. But this ignorance did not cause me much concern. I knew that, once we were face to face together, I should gain the victory over him. And I would be merciless and not falter.

And Jacqueline? If I won, should I not keep her? She was mine, even against her will, by every rule of war. And this was a world of war, where beauty went to the strong, and all rules but that were scratched from the book of life.

I would not even tread softly now, nor slink within the shadows. Nor did I fear Lacroix, although he had fallen out of sight behind me. I strode steadily across the snow and opened the door in the dark wing, entered the hall and ascended the stairway, took the turn to the right and passed through the little hall.

As I had guessed, the light came from Duchaine's room. I heard Leroux's harsh voice within; and if I stopped outside it was not in indecision, but because I meant to make sure of my man this time. Through the crack of the door I saw old Charles Duchaine nodding over his wheel. Leroux was standing near him, and in a corner, beside the window, was Jacqueline. She was facing our common enemy as valiantly as she had done before. And he was still tormenting her.

'I *want* you, Jacqueline,' I heard him say, in a voice which betrayed no throb of passion. 'And I am going to have you. I always have my way. I am not like that weak fool, Hewlett.'

'It was *I* who sent him away, not you,' she cried. 'Do you think he was afraid of you?'

Leroux looked at her in admiration. 'You are a splendid woman, Jacqueline,' he said. 'I like the way you defy me. But you are quite at my mercy. And you are going to yield! You will yield your will to mine — '

'Never!' she cried. 'I will fling myself into the lake before that shall happen. Ah, *monsieur*' — her voice took on a pleading tone — 'why will you not take all we have and let us go? We are two helpless people; we shall never betray your secrets. Why must you have me too?'

'Because I love you, Jacqueline,' he cried passionately. 'I am not a scoundrel. Life is a hard game, and I have played it hard. And I have loved you for a long time, but I would not tell you until I had the right as well as the power!'

He caught her in his arms. She uttered a little gasping cry, and struggled wildly and ineffectually in his grasp. I was quite cold, for I knew that was to be the last of his villainies.

I entered the room and walked up to the table, my pistol raised, aiming at his heart, and I felt my own heart beat steadily, and the will to kill rise dominant above every hesitation.

Leroux spun round. He saw me, and he smiled his sour smile. He did not flinch, although he must have seen that my hand was as steady as a rock. I could not withhold a certain admiration for the man, but this did not weaken me.

'What, you again, *monsieur?*' he asked mockingly. 'You have come back? You are always coming back, aren't you?'

The truth of the diagnosis struck home to me. Yes, I was always coming back. But this time I had come back to stay.

'Can I do anything further for you, M. Hewlett?' he asked. 'Was not your bed comfortable? Do you want something, or is it only habit that has brought you back here where nobody wants you?'

'I have come back to kill you, Leroux,' I answered, and pulled the trigger six times.

And each time I heard nothing but the click of the hammer. Then, with his bull's bellow, Simon was upon me, dashing his fists into my face, and bearing me down. My puny struggles were as ineffective as though I had been fighting ten men. He had me on the floor and was kneeling on my chest, and in a trice the other ruffians had come dashing along the hall.

Jacqueline was beating with her little

fists upon Leroux's broad back, but he did not even feel the blows. I heard old Charles Duchaine's piping cries of fear, and then somebody held me by the throat, and I was swimming in black water.

'Bring a rope, Raoul!' I heard Simon call.

Half-conscious, I knew that I was being tied. I felt the rope tighten upon my wrists and limbs; presently I opened my aching eyes to find myself trussed like a chicken to two legs of the table. I think it was Jean Petitjean who said something about shooting me, and was knocked down for it. Leroux was yelling like a demoniac. I saw Jacqueline's terrified face and the trembling old man; and presently Leroux was standing over me again, perfectly calm. He had taken the pistol from my coat pocket and placed it on the table, and now he took it in his hand and held it under my eyes. The magazine was empty.

'Ah, Paul Hewlett, you are a very poor conspirator indeed,' he said, 'to try to shoot a man without anything in your pistol. Do you remember how affection-ately I put my arm round you when you were sitting in that chair writing your ridiculous cheque? It was then that I took the liberty of extracting the two car-tridges. But I did think you would have had sense to examine your pistol and reload before you returned.'

Jacqueline was clinging to him. '*Mon-sieur*,' she panted, 'you will spare his life? You will unfasten him and let him go?'

'But he keeps coming back,' protested Leroux.

'Spare him, *monsieur*, and God will bless you! You cannot kill him in cold blood,' she cried.

'We will talk about that presently, my dear,' he answered. 'Go and sit down like a good child. I have something more to ask this gentleman before I make my decision.'

He picked up a scrap of newspaper from the table and held it before my eyes, deliberately turning up the oil-lamp wick that I might read it. I recognized it at once. It was the clipping from the newspaper, descriptive of the murdered man, which I had cut out in the train and placed in my pocketbook.

'You dropped this, my friend, when you pulled out your chequebook,' said Simon. 'You are a very poor conspirator, Paul Hewlett. Assuredly I would not have you on my side at any price. Well?'

'Well?' I repeated mechanically.

'Who killed him?' he shouted.

He shook the paper before my eyes and then he struck me across the face with it. '*Who killed Louis d'Epernay?*' he yelled, and Jacqueline screamed in fear.

'I did,' I answered after a moment.

18

The Little Dagger

Leroux staggered back against the wall and stood there, scowling like a devil. It was evident that my answer had been totally unexpected. I had never seen him under the influence of any overwhelming emotion, and I did not at the time understand the cause of his consternation.

Jacqueline was clinging to her father, and the old man looked from one to the other of us in bewilderment, and shook his white head and mumbled.

'Did you — know this, *madame*?' cried Leroux fiercely to Jacqueline.

'Yes,' she replied.

'So this is why you pretended to have forgotten. You remembered everything?'

'Yes.'

'You lied to shield yourself?'

'No, to shield him,' she cried. 'Because

he was my only friend when I was helpless in a strange city. You did not steal my money, did you, Paul?' she added, turning swiftly upon me. 'No, you have paid me. You were keeping it for me.'

'You *lie!*' yelled Leroux, and he struck her across the mouth as he had struck me.

I writhed in my bonds. I pulled the heavy table after me as I tried impotently to crawl toward him, sending the wheel flying and all the papers whirling through the air. I cursed Leroux as blasphemously as he was cursing Jacqueline. I saw a trickle of blood on her cut lip, and the proud smile upon her face as she defied him. And at the door was the pale face of Philippe Lacroix.

Leroux turned on me and kicked me savagely, and dragged the table to the far end of the room, and struck me repeatedly, while I struggled like a madman. There followed a long silence, while Leroux strode furiously about the room. At last he stopped; he seemed to have made up his mind.

'I understand now,' he said, nodding

his head. 'So you are the man who took this woman to the Merrimac. And then to your home, and Louis d'Epernay followed you there, and, naturally, you killed him. Well, it is intelligible. You were not acting for Carson after all, but were infatuated with this woman. Well — but — ' He wheeled and turned to Jacqueline. 'I will marry you still!'

She did not deign to answer him nor to wipe away the blood that trickled down her chin.

'Do you know why?' he bawled.

She raised her eyes indifferently to his. I saw that, though her spirit was unbroken, she was weary to death.

'Because you become part-heir of the seigniory by your husband's death!' he shouted; and then he took Charles Duchaine by the arm and began shaking him violently. 'Listen, you old fool!' he cried. 'Your son-in-law is dead — Louis d'Epernay!'

Charles Duchaine looked at Leroux in his mild way. He had put one arm round his daughter, and he seemed to understand that Simon was maltreating her, and to wish to defend her; but his wits were still wandering, and I saw that he understood only a little of what was passing.

'Louis d'Epernay is dead!' cried Simon, shaking the old man again.

'Well, well!' answered Duchaine, stroking his long beard with his free hand. 'So Louis is dead! Did you kill him, Simon?'

'No, I didn't kill him,' Simon sneered. 'Wake up a little more, Duchaine. Do you know what happens now he is dead?'

'I expect you to get some more money, Simon,' answered the old man with an ingenuousness that made the reply more stinging than any intended irony.

Leroux burst into a mirthless laugh. 'You are quite right, Duchaine,' he answered. 'And I am not going to mince matters. I have a hold over you, and you will do my bidding. You will assign your share to me as your son-in-law.'

I saw Jacqueline looking at me. I would not meet her gaze, but at last her persistence compelled me. Then I saw her glance toward the wall. The two broadswords hung there, within arm's reach, above the broken mirror. My heart leaped up at the thought of her valour. She had no mind to yield! But I shook my head imperceptibly in answer, and looked down at my bonds.

'I don't want you to marry my daughter, Simon,' said old Duchaine mildly. 'I saw you strike her in the face just now. No gentleman would do that. Come, Simon, you know you are not a gentleman; you ought not to think of such a thing. Jacqueline would not be happy with you. What does she say?'

'I don't *care* what she says,' snarled Leroux. 'I will take care of that.'

I had been trying hard to devise some method of freeing myself. My struggles had relaxed the ropes around my wrists sufficiently to allow my hands two or three inches of movement, and I hoped, by hard work, to loosen them sufficiently to enable me to get at least one hand free.

Then I felt that something hard was pressing into my back, just within reach of my right thumb and forefinger. My fur coat, which was still round me, was twisted, so that the inside breast pocket was behind me, and I fancied that the hard object was something that I had placed in this receptacle.

I let my thumb and finger travel up and down it. It had the form of a tiny knife with a heavy rounded handle. And suddenly I knew what it was. It was the knife with which Louis d'Epernay had been killed! I must have put it in my breast pocket at some time, intending to throw it away, and it had slipped through a hole in the lining and gone down as far as the next ridge of fur, where it had become wedged. I could just get my finger and thumb round the point of the blade.

The ropes scored deeply into my wrists as I worked at it, but I felt the lining give, and presently I had worked the blade through and had the knife out by the handle. But it was made for thrusting more than cutting, and I had to pick the ropes to pieces, strand by strand.

Jacqueline had been imperceptibly edging away from her father and Leroux; she was now standing immediately beneath the rusty swords. And outside the door I still perceived Lacroix, motionless. It flashed across my mind that he understood Jacqueline's desperate ruse, and that he was waiting for the issue.

I picked furiously at the ropes which bound my hands, and a long strand uncoiled and whipped back on my wrist. Suddenly I heard old Charles Duchaine bring down his fist with a vigorous thud upon the end of the table. 'I'll see you in Hell first, Simon!' was his unexpected remark.

'What?' cried Simon, taken completely aback.

'No, Simon,' continued the old man in his mild voice once more. 'You are not a gentleman, you know, and you are not fit to marry Jacqueline.'

Leroux thrust his hard face into the old man's. 'Duchaine, your wits are wandering,' he answered. 'Listen now! Have you forgotten that the government is searching for you night and day? It was a long time ago that you killed a soldier of the Canadian forces, but not too long ago for the government to remember. It has a long memory and a long arm, too, and at a word from me — ' It was pitiful to see the change that came over Duchaine's face. He shook with fear and stretched out his withered hands appealingly.

'Simon, you wouldn't betray me after all these years of friendship?' he cried. '*Mon Dieu*, I do not wish to hang!'

'Keep calm, Charles, my friend,' responded Simon glibly. 'I am ready to return friendship for friendship. Will you acknowledge me as your son-in-law and heir?'

'Yes,' stammered the old man. 'Take everything, Simon; only leave me free.'

'Well, that is more reasonable,' said Leroux, evidently mollified. 'I am not the man to go back on my friends. I shall give you a cash return of ten thousand dollars. You have not forgotten the old times in Quebec?'

'No, Simon,' muttered Duchaine, looking up hopefully at him.

'If you had ten thousand dollars, Charles, you could make your fortune in a week. They play high nowadays, and your system would sweep all before it.'

'Yes, yes!' cried the dotard eagerly. 'If

only I had ten thousand dollars I could make my fortune. But I am old now. My little daughter has gone to New York to play for me. You did not know that, Simon, did you?' he added, looking at him with a cunning leer.

'She cannot play as well as you, Charles,' said Leroux. 'You have played so long, you know; you have the system at your fingertips. There is nobody who could stand up against you. Do you remember Louis Street and the fine people who were your friends? How they will welcome you! You could become a man of fashion again, in spite of your long exile in these solitudes. Do you recollect the races, where thousands can be won in a few minutes, when your horse romps home by a neck? And the gaming tables, where a thousand dollars is but a pinch of dust, and the bright lights and the chink of money — and you winning it all away? You can have horses and carriages again, and all houses will be open to you, for your little error has long ago been forgotten. And you are not an old man, Charles.'

'Yes, yes, Simon!' cried the old man, fascinated by the picture. 'It is worth it — by gracious, it is!'

Jacqueline swung round on Leroux. I saw her fists clench and her bruised lip quiver. 'Never, Simon Leroux!' she said. 'And, what is more, my father is not competent to transfer his property, and I will fight you through every court in the land.'

'I was coming to you, *madame*,' sneered Simon. 'I don't know much about the courts in this part of the country, but you will marry me to save the life of your lover.'

'No!' she answered, setting her teeth. He seized her by the wrists and dragged her across the floor to me.

'Look at him!' he yelled. 'Look into his face. Will you marry me if I let him go free?'

'No!' answered Jacqueline.

'I swear to you that he shall be thrown from the top of the cataract unless you give your consent within five minutes.'

'Never!' she answered firmly.

'I will denounce your father!'

238

'You can't frighten me with such stuff. I am not a weak old man!'

'You will think differently after Charles Duchaine has been hanged in Quebec jail,' he sneered.

His words received a wholly unexpected answer. The dotard leaped forward, stooped down, and picked up the heavy roulette-wheel. He raised it aloft and staggered wildly toward Leroux.

19

The Hidden Chamber

Simon turned just in time. The wheel went crashing to the floor and bounded and rebounded out of the room and along the little hall. Philippe jumped in terror from the place where he crouched. And then the last strand broke, and I was free to slip the cords from my limbs.

'You old fool!' screamed Leroux, catching Duchaine by the wrists. But Charles Duchaine possessed the strength of a madman. He grasped Leroux round the waist and clung to him, and would not be shaken off.

'Kill him!' he screamed. 'He is a spy! He has come to betray me to the government!'

What followed was the work of a moment. I saw Jacqueline pull down both broadswords from the wall. She flung one down beside me just as I was staggering to my feet.

Leroux shook off the old man at last. He turned on me. I swung the sword aloft and brought it down upon his skull. Heaven knows I struck to kill; but my wrist was feeble from the ropes, and the blade fell flat. It drew no blood, but Leroux dropped like a stricken ox upon the floor.

'This way!' gasped the old man. He pulled at Jacqueline's arm, and half-led and half-dragged her through the open door behind his chair, I following. Lacroix sprang into the room and called, but whether to us or to the other ruffians I did not know. Leroux sat up and looked about him, dazed and bewildered.

Then I was in the little room with Jacqueline and Duchaine, and he turned and bolted the door behind us. He seemed possessed of all the strength and decision of youth again.

When I stood there before the room had been as dark as pitch, but now a flicker of light was at the far end. A voice cried: '*M'sieur! M'sieur!* I have not forgotten thee!'

It was Pierre Caribou. I saw his figure

silhouetted against the light of the flaring candle which he held in his hand.

Duchaine had placed one arm about his daughter's waist, and was urging her along. But she stopped and looked back to me. I saw she held one broadsword in her hand, as I held the other. 'Come, monsieur!' she gasped.

But I was too mad with the desire to make an end of Leroux to accompany her. I wanted to go back. I tried to find the bolt of the door in the gloom, but while my fingers were fumbling for it Jacqueline came running back to me.

'Quick, or we are lost!' she cried.

'I am going back,' I answered, still fumbling for the bolt Duchaine had drawn.

'No! We are safe inside. It is a secret room. My father made it in the first days of his sojourn here in case he was pursued, and none but Pierre and he know the secret. Ah, come, monsieur — come!' She clung to me desperately, and there was an intensity of entreaty in her voice.

I hesitated. There was no sound in the

room without, and I believed that the two ruffianly followers were ignorant of what had happened, and had not dared to return after being driven away.

But I meant to kill Leroux, and still felt for the bolt. As I fumbled there, the door splintered suddenly, and Jacqueline cried out. Through the hole I saw the oil lamp shining in the outer room. The door splintered again. All at once I realized that Leroux was firing his revolver at the panels. It was fortunate that we both stood at one side, where the latch was.

Then I yielded reluctantly to Jacqueline's soft violence. I followed her through the dark chamber, under an archway of stone, and through a winding passage in the rock. Pierre's candle flickered before us, and in another moment we had squeezed through a narrow opening into a chamber in the cliff.

On the ground were five or six large stones, and Pierre began to fit them into the aperture through which we had passed. In a minute the place was completely sealed, and we four stood and looked breathlessly at one another within what might have been a cenotaph. Not the slightest sound came from without.

We were standing in a stone chamber, apparently of natural formation, but finished with rough masonry work. It was about the size of a large room, and I could see that it was only a widening of the tunnel itself, which continued through a narrow exit at the farther end, running on into the unknown depths of the cliff. From the freshness of the air, I inferred that it connected with the surface at no distant place.

The entrance through which we had come had been made by blasting at some period, or widened in this way, and then cemented, for the stones which Pierre had fitted into it exactly filled it, so that it was barely distinguishable from where I stood, and I am certain that it would have required a prolonged scrutiny on the part of searchers on the outside to enable them to detect it. And even then only dynamite or blasting powder could have forced a path, and it would have been exceedingly difficult to handle such materials within the tunnel without blocking the approach completely, while leaving open the farther exit.

The chamber seemed at one time to have been prepared for such a contingency as had occurred, for there were wool rugs on the stone floor, though they had rotted and partly disintegrated from the dampness. There were a table and wooden chairs, also partially decayed. The mouldering fringes of some rugs protruded from a bundle wrapped in oil paper.

Pierre Caribou opened this and shook them out on the ground. Except where their edges had been exposed, they were in good condition, and were thick enough to lie upon without much discomfort. The interior of the cave was pleasantly warm, though moist.

'M. Duchaine made this place in case gov'ment men came to take him,' explained Pierre as he placed the rugs on the floor. 'No can find, no can break down the stone door. Simon does not know — only *m'sieur* and me. I came that way; I saw you tied and knew it was time to come here. Soon the time to kill Simon will come as well.'

'When in Heaven's name will it come?' I cried.

'Soon. His *diable* has told me,' answered Pierre Caribou.

The chamber was as silent as the grave, except for the gurgling of a spring of water somewhere and the occasional pattering fall of a drop of moisture from the roof. And truly this might prove our grave, I thought, and none would find our bones in this heart of the cliff through all the ages that would come.

The flight seemed to have exhausted the last flicker of vitality in the old man, for he sank down upon the blankets in a somnolent condition. I could readily understand how his perpetual fear of discovery, intensified through many years of solitude, had grown to be an obsession, and how Leroux's idle threats had stimulated his weakened will to one last effort to escape.

Jacqueline knelt by his side. She paid no attention to me, except that once she asked for water. Pierre brought her some from the spring in a tin cup, and when she raised her head I could see that her lip was swollen from the blow of Leroux's fist.

The old man's hands were moving restlessly. Jacqueline bent over him and whispered, and he stirred and cried out petulantly. He missed his roulette-wheel, his constant companion through those years, his coins, and paper. In his way perhaps he was suffering the most of all.

'I will go now,' Pierre announced. Tomorrow I will come for you, and take all through the tunnel. You stay here till I come; sleep till morning.'

'I will go with you, Pierre,' I said, still under my obsession. But he laid his heavy hand upon my arm and pushed me away.

'You did not kill Simon,' he answered. 'Why did you not kill him when you had the sword? Only a *diable* can kill him. When the time comes, the *diable* will tell me. You sleep now. I will take my woman safe through the tunnel to a place I know. When my woman is safe, I will come back to you.'

It was a brave and simple declaration of first principles, and none the less affecting, because it came from the lips of a faithful, ignorant old man. It was just such simple loyalty that natures like Leroux's never knew, frustrating the most cunning plans based on self-interest.

I realized the strength of Pierre's argument. His duty lay first toward his kin; then he would place his life at his master's service. But he would have to cover many miles before he returned. He went without a backward glance; but I saw his throat heave, and I knew what the parting meant to him. The feudal loyalty of the past was all his faith.

I flung myself down on my blanket. I was utterly exhausted, and with that dead weariness which precludes sleep. The candle was burning low and was guttering down upon one side, and a pool of hardening grease was spreading over the table-top.

I walked over to the table and blew it out. We must husband it; the darkness in the cave would become unbearable without a candle to light. I lay down again. The silence was loneliness itself, and not rendered less lonely by the occasional cries of the old man and the drip, drip of water. I could not see anything, and Jacqueline might have been a woman of stone, for she made not the least movement. But I felt her presence; I seemed to feel her thoughts, to live in her. At last I spoke to her.

'Jacqueline!'

I heard her start, and knew that she had raised her head and was looking after me. I crawled toward her, dragging my blanket after me. I felt in the darkness for the place where I knew her hand must be and took it in mine.

'Jacqueline,' I said, 'you know I did not steal your money, don't you?'

'Forgive me, *monsieur*,' I heard her whisper.

'Forgive *me*, Jacqueline, for I have brought heavy trouble upon you. But with God's aid, I am going to save you both — your father and you — and take you away somewhere where all the past can be forgotten.'

She sighed heavily, and I felt a tear drop on my hand.

'Jacqueline!' I cried.

'Ah, M. Hewlett' — the weariness of

her voice went to my heart — 'it might have been different — if — '

'If what, Jacqueline?'

'If there had not been the blood of a dead man between us,' she moaned. 'If — you — had not — killed him!'

Her words were a revelation to me, for I learned that she had mercifully been spared the full remembrance of what had happened in the Tenth Street apartment. She thought that it was I who had killed Louis d'Epernay. And how could I deny this, when to do so would be to bring to her mind the knowledge of her own dreadful guilt?

The dotard stirred and muttered, and she whispered to him and soothed him as though he were a child. Presently he began to breathe heavily, as old men breathe in sleep. But Jacqueline crouched there in the same motionless silence, and I knew that she was awake and suffering.

My mind was working against my will and picturing a thousand possibilities. What was Leroux doing? He would act with his usual hammer force. All depended on Pierre.

The hours wore away, and we three lay

there, two waiting and one dreaming of the old days of youth, no doubt. I tried to light the candle to see the time, but my shaking hand sent it flying across the cave, and when I searched for my matches, I found that the box was empty.

It seemed an eternity since we had come there. It is one thing to wait for dawn and quite another thing to wait where dawn will never come.

It must be day. And still Pierre did not come. As I lay there, listening for his returning footsteps, I heard Jacqueline breathe at last. She was asleep from weariness after her long night's watch. Somehow the thought that she had passed into the world of dreams comforted me. For a brief time the dreadful accusation of murder had been lifted from my head, and my numbed mind was free to follow my will and leave its mad career of fancy. I could act now.

Why should I not follow where Pierre had led? If Leroux had captured him within his hut, as seemed only too likely, he would never return, and we should wait in vain. And with each hour of waiting our chances to escape grew less.

I resolved to follow the exit for a little distance to see whither it led, and if I could discover the light of day.

So I took my sword and sallied out through the passage in the cliff

20

At Swords' Points

I entered the tunnel, sword in hand, keeping both arms stretched out to feel my way. I resolved that I would always keep the left hand in contact with the wall upon that side, so that, in case the tunnel should divide, by reversing the process I could ensure my safe return.

I had only proceeded a few steps when the air grew cold and sweet. And before I had traversed two hundred yards, I saw a dim light in the distance. So I had endured all those agonies of mind with the open air but a short distance away!

As I advanced, I fancied that I heard the soft pattering of feet behind me. I crouched against the wall and waited, listening intently. But I heard nothing except the distant roaring of the cataracts. How sweet they sounded now!

I leant against the wall and facing

backward, holding my sword ready to meet any intruder. But there was no sound from within, except the soughing which one hears in a tunnel; and satisfied at last that I had been my imagination, I pursued my course.

The light slowly grew brighter, until all at once I saw what seemed to be the gleam of an electric arc-light immediately ahead. It dazzled and half-blinded me.

I started backward; and then the noble morning star disclosed herself, swinging in the sky like a blazing jewel in a translucent sea. Before me was a projecting piece of rock, which had shut off the view, and but for that warning star I must have gone to my death: for my foot was slipping on ice — and I was clinging to the cliff-wall upon the other side of the tiny platform, where I had stood with Pierre, and the Old Angel thundered over me. And, instead of noon, as I had thought it to be, it was only dawn, and the distant sky was banded with faint bars of yellow and gold, and the fresh morning air was in my nostrils.

I picked my way back, inch by inch,

across the ice which coated the rocky floor for a few yards within the tunnel, until I stood in safety again.

The full purport of this discovery now came to me. Since the cave connected with that platform beneath the cataract, it was evident that by crossing the ledge, a dangerous but not precarious feat, I should enter the main tunnel again and come out eventually beyond the hills, even allowing for a preliminary blunder into the wrong track.

The greatest danger lay in the possibility of Leroux or his aids lying in wait for me somewhere within the tunnel, and I had not much fear of that, for I did not believe they suspected that our cave connected with the main passage. It was more likely that they would wait in Duchaine's room till hunger drove us out.

So I started back to Jacqueline. But I had not gone six paces before I heard a scream that still rings in my ears today, and a shadow sprang out of the darkness and rushed at me. It was old Charles Duchaine. His white hair streamed behind him; his face bore an expression of indelible horror and rage, and in his hand he held the other sword. With a madman's proverbial cunning he had pretended to be asleep; then he must have followed me stealthily as I made my journey of exploration; and now, doubtless, he ascribed all his wrongs and sufferings to me and meant to kill me.

His fears had snapped the last frail link that bound him to the world of sense. He struck at me, a great sweeping blow which would almost have cut me in two. I had just time to parry it, and then he was upon me, raining blows upon my outstretched sword. He was no swordsman, but slashed and hewed in frenzy, and the steel rang on steel, and the rust from the blades filled my nostrils with its sting.

But, though his attack was wild, the vigor of his blows almost beat down my guard. At last a random blow of mine swept the weapon from his feeble old hand and sent it whirling down the cataract into the lake below. Then he was at my throat, and it was fortunate that there was firm rock instead of slippery ice beneath us, or we should both have followed the sword.

He linked his arms around me and wrestled furiously, and his weight and height so much surpassed my own that they compensated for his weakness. We swayed backward and forward, and the star dipped and swung over us, as though we stood upon the deck of a rolling ship.

'Calm yourself, for Heaven's sake, *monsieur*!' I gasped as I gained a momentary advantage over him. 'Don't you know me? I am your friend. I want to save you!'

But he was at me again, trying to lock his hands about my throat; and, even after I had controlled him and pinned his arms to his sides, he fought like a fiend, and never ceased to yell.

'You shall not take me! I have done nothing! It was years ago! Let me go! Let me go!' he screamed.

I released him for a moment, hoping that his disordered brain would calm enough for him to recognize me. But suddenly, with a final howl, he sprang past me, sweeping me against the wall, and leaped out on the ledge.

I held my breath. I expected to see him stagger to his death below. But he stood motionless in the middle of the little platform and stretched out his arms toward the raging torrent, as though in invocation. Then he leaped across with the agility of a wild sheep and rushed on into the tunnel beyond. I drew my breath thickly and leaned against the wall, overcome with nausea. The physical shock of the struggle was, however, less appalling than the thought of Jacqueline.

I had no hope that the old man would ever return, or that his crazed brain remembered the way home to the cave. He would wander on through the tunnels, either to perish in them miserably, or to emerge at last into the snow beyond and die there. Unless Leroux found him.

I started back, keeping this time to the right side of the tunnel, until I heard the gurgling of the brook. Then I heard Jacqueline's footstep.

'Who is it?' she called wildly. 'M. Hewlett! My father — !'

I caught her as she swayed toward me.

'He has gone, Jacqueline,' I said. 'I went into the tunnel to try to find the way. He had been feigning sleep, and he crept after me. I tried to stop him. He was so frightened that I thought it best to let him go. He ran on into the tunnel — '

'We must find him,' she said.

'He will come back, Jacqueline.'

'He will *never* come back!' she answered. 'He must have been planning this and waiting for me to sleep. For years he brooded over his danger, suspecting everybody, and the shock of last night unhinged his mind. He may be hiding somewhere. We must search for him.'

'Let us go, then, Jacqueline,' I answered.

In fact, there seemed to be no use in remaining any longer. If Pierre were on his way back, we ought to meet him in the tunnel; and if he had been captured, delay spelled ruin.

So I led her back into the tunnel on what was to be, I hoped, our final journey. We reached the ledge. The star had faded now, and the whole sky was bright with the red clouds of dawn. Very cautiously we picked our way across the platform, clinging to the wall. It was a hideous journey over the slippery ice, beneath the thunder of the cataract; and when at length we reached the tunnel on the other side, I was shaking like a man with a palsy. But, thank God, that nightmare was past. And with renewed confidence I went on through the darkness, with Jacqueline at my side, feeling my way by the deeper depression in the ground along the centre of the tubular passage.

At length I saw daylight ahead of me — and there was no sound of the torrents. Fortune had led us where I had wanted her to lead — into the open space where the gold was. From there I knew that I could strike the passage which led into the sleigh road under the hills. Half an hour's travel ought to bring us to the rocking stone at the entrance, and safety. But I found that I had entered the mine from a third point, and that some forty feet away from the place where I had emerged before. This time we were inside the cave in which Leroux and Lacroix had piled the sacks of earth.

I was looking out beyond them toward

the rivulet, and on my right hand and on my left the tunnel stretched away, leading respectively toward the *château* and to the rocking stone at the entrance.

I left Jacqueline in the cave for a few moments and went into the smaller one nearby, where I had seen the provisions on the preceding day. I found a small box of hard biscuit, with which I stuffed the pockets of my coat, and, happier still, a small revolver and some cartridges, to which I helped myself liberally. Then I went back to Jacqueline.

We must go on. Half an hour more should see us outside the tunnel beyond the mountains. And this was the day on which Père Antoine would be expecting me. It seemed incredible that so much could have happened in four-and-twenty hours. But there was no sign of Charles Duchaine. And I did not intend to jeopardize our future for the sake of the crazed old man.

'Jacqueline,' I said, 'let us go on. Perhaps your father is on his way outside the tunnel.'

She shook her head. 'We must find him

first,' she answered.

'But that is impossible,' I protested. 'How can we go wandering among these dark passages when we do not know where he has gone? You know he is invaluable to Leroux, and he will come to no harm with him. If we get free, we can return with aid and rescue him.'

'We cannot go without my father,' she answered, shaking her head in determination.

'But — '

'Oh, don't you see that we *must* find him?' she cried wildly. '*But you* must go. You cannot be burdened with me. Give up your hopeless mission to rescue us, *monsieur*, and save yourself!'

At that my hopes, which had been so high, went crashing down.

'Jacqueline,' I said, 'if we can find your father, you will come with me? Because it has occurred to me,' I went on, 'that if he had come this way, his footprints would be in the mud beside the stream. It would take an hour or two for them to fill up again. So perhaps he did not come this far, but is hiding in some cave in the tunnel through which we came. Will you wait for me here while I go back and search?'

She nodded, and I went back into that interminable tunnel again.

21

The Bait That Lured

I went along the tunnel in the direction of *le Vieil Ange*. It was broad day now, and the distance between the cataract and the open ground where the gold had been mined was sufficiently short for the whole length of the passage to be faintly visible. It was a reach of deep twilight, brightening into sunlight at either end.

I picked my way carefully, peering into the numerous small caves and fissures in the wall on either hand. And I was about halfway through when I saw a shadow running in front of me and making no sound.

It was Duchaine. There could be no mistaking that tall, gaunt figure, just visible against the distant day. He was running in his bare feet and, therefore, in complete silence, and he leaped across the rocky floor as though he wore moccasins.

I raced along the tunnel after him. But he seemed to be endowed with the speed of a deer, for he kept his distance easily, and I would never have caught him had he not stopped for an instant at the approach of the ledge. There, just as he was poising himself to leap, I seized him by the arm.

'M. Duchaine! M. Duchaine! Stop!' I implored him. 'Don't you know that I am your friend — your daughter Jacqueline's friend? I want to save you!'

He did not attempt violence, but gazed at me with hesitation and pathetic doubt. 'They want to catch me,' he muttered. 'They want to hang me. He has got a gallows ready for me to swing on, because I killed a soldier in the Fenian raids. But it wasn't I,' he added with sudden cunning. 'It was my brother, who looks like me. He died long ago. Let me go, *monsieur*. I am a poor, harmless old man. I shall not hurt anybody.'

I took his hand in mine. 'M. Duchaine,' I answered, 'I am your friend; I want to save you, not capture you. Come back with me, *monsieur*, and I will take you away — '

The wild look came into his eyes again. 'No, no!' he screamed, trying to wrest himself from my grasp and measuring the distance across the ledge with his eye. 'I will not go away. This is my home. I want to live here in peace. I want my wheel! *Monsieur*, give me my wheel. I have perfected a system. Listen!' He took me by the arm and spoke in that cunning madman's way: 'I will make your fortune if you will let me go free. We will go to Quebec together and play at the tables, as I did when I was a young man. My system cannot fail!'

'M. Duchaine,' I pleaded, 'won't you come back with me and let us talk it over? Jacqueline is with me — '

'You can't catch me with such a trick as that. My little daughter has gone to New York to make our fortunes at M. Daly's gaming-house. She will be back soon, loaded down with gold.'

I saw an opening here. 'She has come back,' I answered. 'She is not fifty yards away.'

'With gold?' he inquired, looking at me doubtfully.

'With gold,' I answered, trying to allure his imagination as Leroux had done. 'She has rich gold, red gold, such as you will love. You can take up the coins in your fingers and let the gold stream slip through them. Come with me, *monsieur.*'

I grasped him by the arm and tried to lead him with me. My argument had moved him; I thought I had won him. But just as I started back into the tunnel, a pebble leaped from the rocky platform and rebounded from the cliff. I cast a backward glance, and there upon the opposite side I saw Leroux standing.

There was something appalling in the man's presence there. I think it was his unchanging and implacable pursuit that for the moment daunted me. And this was symbolized in his fur coat, which he wore open in the front exactly as he had worn it that day when we met in the New York store, and as I had always seen him wear it.

He stood bareheaded, and his massive, lined, hard, weather-beaten face might have been a sneering gargoyle's, carved out of granite on some cathedral wall. His aspect so fascinated me that I forgot my resolution to shoot to kill.

'Bonjour, M. Hewlett,' he called across the chasm. 'Don't be afraid of me any more than I am afraid of you. Just wait a moment. I want to talk business.'

'I have no business to talk with you,' I answered.

'Not with you, *monsieur*,' he sneered. 'It is with our friend, Duchaine!'

At the sound of Leroux's voice, the old man began muttering and looking from one to the other of us undecidedly. I tried to drag him within the tunnel, but he shook himself free and sprang out on the icy ledge. He poised himself there, turning his head from side to side as either of us spoke. And he effectively prevented me from shooting Leroux.

'Don't you know your best friends, Duchaine?' inquired Leroux; and the white beard was tipped toward the other side of the ledge.

'I don't know who my friends are, Simon,' answered Duchaine in his mild, melancholy voice. 'What do you want?'

'Why, I want you, Charles, my old

friend,' replied Leroix. 'You old fool, do you want to die? If you do, go with that man. He comes from Quebec on government business.'

But I could plead better than that. I knew the symbol in his imagination. 'M. Duchaine! Come with me! He has a gallows ready for you back in that tunnel!'

I saw Duchaine start violently and cling to the icy wall. 'No, no!' he cried; 'I won't go with *either* of you. I am a poor old man. It was my brother who shot the soldier, and he is dead. Go away!' He burst into senile tears and cowered there. The memories of the past thronged around him like avenging demons.

Suddenly I saw him turn his head and fix his eyes upon Leroux. He craned his neck forward; and then, very slowly, he began to walk toward his persecutor. I craned my own neck. Leroux was holding out — the roulette-wheel!

'Come along, Charles, my friend,' he cried. 'Come, let us try our fortunes! Don't you want to stake some money upon your system against me?'

The old figure leaped forward over the

ledge, and in a moment Leroux had grasped him and pulled him into the tunnel. I whipped my revolver out and sent shot after shot across the chasm. The sound of the discharges echoed and re-echoed along the tunnel wall. But the projecting ledge of rock effectively screened Leroux — and Duchaine as well, for in my passion I had been firing blindly, and but for that I should undoubtedly have killed Jacqueline's father.

The mocking laughter of Leroux came back to me in faint and far-away reply. I saw the explanation of the man's presence now. He must have met Duchaine that morning as the old man was flying or wandering aimlessly along the tunnel. They had reached *le Vieil Ange* together, and Leroux had probably had little difficulty in inducing the witless old man to take him back into the secret hiding-place. It was lucky that we had not been there when Leroux discovered it. We must have crossed the ledge only a moment or two before them.

I hastened back to Jacqueline, and encountered her in the passage just where the light and darkness blended, standing with arms stretched out against the wall to steady herself.

'Oh, I thought you were dead!' she sobbed, and fell into my arms.

I held her tightly to support her, and I led her back to the gold cave. In a few words I explained what had occurred.

'Now, Jacqueline, you must let me guide you,' I said. 'There is no chance for us unless we leave your father for the present where he is and make our own escape. We can reach Père Antoine's cabin soon after midday, and we can tell him your father is a prisoner here. He would not come with us, Jacqueline, even if he were here. And if he did, he might escape us on the way and wander back into the tunnels again. Leroux has no cause to harm him. He needs his signature to the deed which is to give him your father's share of the seigniory. Just as he wants you, Jacqueline. So I shall not let you go back, or he would get you in the end. Unless — '

'Unless I kill myself,' she answered wildly. 'That is the best way out, Paul! I

271

am fated to bring nothing but evil upon everyone with whom I come in contact. Ah, leave me, Paul, and save yourself!'

Again I pleaded, and she did not respond. She was so silent that I thought I had convinced her. I urged her to her feet. But suddenly I heard a stealthy footfall close at hand, between the cave and the cataract.

I placed my finger on Jacqueline's lips and crept stealthily to the passage, revolver in hand. Then, in the gloom, I saw the villainous face of Jean Petitjean looking into mine, twelve paces away, and in his hand was a revolver, too. We fired together. But the surprise spoiled his aim, for his bullet whistled past me. I think my shot struck him somewhere, for he uttered a yell and began running back along the tunnel as hard as he could.

I followed him, firing as fast as I could reload. But there was a slight bend in the passage here, and my bullets only struck the walls. When I reached the light, he was scrambling across the ledge, and before I could cover him he had succeeded in disappearing behind the projecting rock on the other side.

So Leroux had already sealed one exit — that by the Old Angel, where the road led into the main passage. Had he had time to reach the exit by the mine?

I ran back at full speed to the cave. 'Jacqueline!' I called. She did not answer.

I ran forward and saw her near the earth-sacks, lying upon her side. Her eyes were closed, her face as white as a dead woman's.

White — but her dress was blood-soaked, and there was blood on the sacks and on the stony floor. It oozed from her side, and her hand was cold as the rocks, and there was no flutter at her wrist.

The bullet from Jean Petitjean's revolver that missed me must have penetrated her body. She lived, for her breast stirred, though so faintly that it seemed as though all that remained of life were concentrated in the faintly throbbing heartbeats. I raised her in my arms and placed a sack beneath her head, making a resting place for her with my fur coat. Then with my knife I cut away her dress over the wound. There was a bullet hole beneath her breast, stained with dark blood. I ran down to the rivulet, risking an ambuscade, brought back cold water, and washed it, and stanched the flow as best I could, making a bandage and placing it above the wound.

It was a poor effort at first aid, by one who had never seen a bullet-wound before, and I was distracted with misery and grief; and yet I remember how steady my hands were and with what precision and care I performed my task. I have a dim remembrance of losing my self-control when this was done, and clasping her in my arms and pressing my lips to her cold cheek and begging her to live and praying wildly that she should not die. Then I raised her in my arms and was staggering across the cave toward the tunnel which led to the rocking stone.

22

Surrender

I saw the light, the sun's rays bright on the cliff tops. Once in the tunnel beyond that I could keep my pursuers at bay with my revolver, even if I had to fight every inch of my way to freedom. And then, just as I approached the barricade of earth-filled bags, Leroux and the man Raoul emerged from the tunnel's mouth and ran toward me.

If I had been alone and unencumbered, I believe I could have run across the open and won free. But with Jacqueline in my arms it was impossible. I stopped behind the barricade. Even so, I was fortunate, for had they gained the cave before I did, they would have had me at their mercy like a rat trapped in a hole. They saw me and drew back hastily within the tunnel's mouth. I was panting with the weight of my unconscious burden, and I did not know what to do. My mind was filled with rage against my fate, and I shouted curses at them and from behind the bags.

Presently I saw something white fluttering from the tunnel. It was a white handkerchief upon a stick of wood, and slowly and gingerly Raoul emerged into the open. At that instant I fired. The bullet whipped past his face, and with an oath he dropped the stick and handkerchief too, and scuttled back to shelter. Then Leroux's voice hailed me from the tunnel.

'Hewlett!' he called, and there was no trace of mockery in his tones now. 'Will you come out and talk with me? Will you meet me in the open, if you prefer?'

I fired another shot in futile rage. It struck the cliff and sent a stone flying into the stream.

Then silence followed. And I took Jacqueline and carried her back into the little hollow place. I put my hand upon her breast. It stirred. She breathed faintly, though she showed no sign of consciousness.

And then I acted as a trapped animal

would act. I raged up and down the tunnel from cataract to cave, and at each end I fired wildly, though there was no sign of any guard. Why should their guards expose themselves to fire at me when they had me at their mercy? They could surprise me from either end, and I suppose I thought by this trick to maintain the illusion of having some companion. Heaven knows what was in my mind. But now I stood beneath that awful cataract firing at the blind rock, and now I was back behind the earth-bags shooting into the tunnel. And again I was at Jacqueline's side, crouching over her, imploring her to open her eyes once more and speak to me.

So the afternoon wore away. The sun had sunk behind the cliffs. I had fired away all but six of my cartridges. Then the memory of my similar act of folly before came home to me. I understood Leroux's intentions — he meant to surprise me in the night when I was worn out, or when I made a blind dash in the dark for the tunnel.

I felt my way around the cave with the

faint hope that there might be some other egress there. There was none, but I made out a recess which I had not perceived, about one-half as large as the cave itself, and opening into it by a small passage just large enough to give admittance to a single person. Here I should have only one front to defend.

So I carried Jacqueline inside and began laboriously to drag the bags of earth into this last refuge. Before it had grown quite dark, I had barricaded Jacqueline and myself within a place enclosed upon three sides with rock. And there I waited for the end.

I heard the gurgle of the stream and the slow drip of water from the rocks, but nothing more. The starlight was just bright enough to prevent an absolute surprise.

But I was utterly fatigued. I sat beside Jacqueline, holding her hand with one of mine, and my revolver in the other. There was a faint flutter at her wrist. I fancied that it had grown stronger during the past half-hour. But I was unprepared to hear her whisper to me, and when she spoke I was alert in a moment.

'Paul!' she said faintly. 'Bend down. I want to speak to you. I have been conscious for a long time . . . '

'My dear!' was all that I could say. I clasped her cold little hand tightly in mine.

'I don't know whether I shall live, Paul,' she went on. 'But now things have become much clearer. When you wanted to take me through the tunnel, I knew that you were wrong. I knew that even if we found my father, I must still send you away, my dear. Don't you see why? It is because there is the blood of a dead man between us that cannot be wiped away. That is the cause of our misfortunes here, and they will never end, even if you can beat Leroux — because of that. So it could never have been . . . '

Her voice broke off from weakness, and my eyes searched the space beyond the bags. How long would they delay?

Presently Jacqueline spoke again. 'Do you know, Paul, I don't think life is such a good thing as it used to seem,' she said. 'I think I could yield to Leroux and be his wife to save your life.'

'No, Jacqueline.'

'Yes, Paul. If I live, my duty is with my father. And, though he might come to no harm, I cannot leave him. And you must leave me, Paul, because of what is between us. You must go to Leroux and tell him so. You love me, Paul?'

'Always, Jacqueline,' I whispered.

She put her arms about my neck. 'I love you, too,' she said. 'I have always remembered a good deal more than you believed. Only I would not let myself remember anything except that I had you. And do you know what I admired and loved you for, even when you thought my mind unstable and empty? How true you were! That was why, when I remembered everything that dreadful night in the snow, the revulsion was so terrible. I ran away in horror. I could not believe that it was true — and yet I knew it was.

'And Leroux was waiting there and found me. I did not want to leave you, but he told me there was Père Antoine's cabin close by, and that you would come to no harm. And he said you had stolen my money as well. But I never believed that, and I only taunted you with it to drive you away for your own sake.'

She drew me weakly toward her and went on: 'Bend lower . . . nearer. Do you remember, in the train going to Quebec — I lay awake all night and cried, at first for happiness, to think you loved me, and then for shame, because I had no right — though I did not remember who he was at the time, the shock had been so great. That night, lying in my berth, I was shameless. I slipped the wedding ring from my finger and hid it away so that you should not know — because I loved you. And now that we are to part forever, and perhaps I am to die, I can speak to you from my heart. Kiss me — as though I were your wife, Paul.'

She added presently, 'So you will go to Leroux?'

'Is that your will, Jacqueline?'

'Yes. We have fought and now we are beaten.'

I bowed my head. I knew that she spoke the truth. Even though, by some miracle, the tunnel lay clear before us, to move her meant her death. So I would yield, to save her life, and with me Leroux might deal as he chose.

So I left her and climbed across the bags and went down toward the stream. But before I had reached it, a dark figure slipped from among the shadows of the rocks and came toward me; and by the faint starlight I saw the face of Pierre Caribou!

He stopped me and held me by both shoulders, and he drew me into the recesses of the rocks and bent his wizened old face forward toward mine.

'Ah, *monsieur*, so you did not obey old Pierre Caribou and stay in the cave,' he said.

'Pierre, I did not know that you would return,' I answered. 'I thought that we could find the same road that you had taken.'

'Never mind,' the Indian answered, looking at me strangely. 'All finished now. The *diable* will take Leroux. His time has come. The *diable* showed me!'

'How?' I answered, startled.

'All finished,' said Pierre inexorably,

and, as I watched him, a superstitious fear crept over me. He who had cringed even when he gave the command, now cringed no longer, and there was a look on his old face that I had only seen on one man's before — on my father's, the night he died.

'Pierre, where is Leroux?' I whispered.

'No matter,' he answered. 'All finished now.'

'Shall I surrender to him, or shall I fight?'

'No matter,' he said once again. '*M'sieur*, suppose you go back to *ma'm 'selle*, and soon Simon will come. His *diable* will lead him to you. His *diable* will tell you what to say. All finished now!'

He walked past me noiselessly, a tenuous shadow, and his bearing was as proud as that of his race from long ago. He entered the passage at the back of the mine, through which I had come when I encountered Lacroix the first time with his gold.

I went back to Jacqueline and took my seat upon the earth-bag barricade. I had my revolver in my hand, but it was not loaded. I threw the cartridges upon the floor. It seemed only a few minutes before a voice hailed me from the tunnel.

'M. Hewlett! Are you prepared to speak with M. Leroux?'

It was Raoul's voice, and I answered yes.

A moment later Leroux came from the tunnel toward me. I got down from the barricade and met him at the stream. He stood upon the other side, and the stream gurgled and played between us.

'Paul Hewlett,' said Leroux, 'you have made a good fight. By God, you have fought well! But you are done for. I offer you the same terms as before.'

'You planned to murder me,' I answered, but with no bitterness.

'Yes, that is true,' answered Leroux. 'But circumstances were different then from what they are tonight. I am no murderer; I am a man of business. And, within business limits, I keep my word. If I proposed to break it, it was because I had no other way. Besides, you had me in your power. Now you are in mine.

'I thought then that you were in

Carson's pay. That if I let you go you would betray . . . certain things you might have discovered. But you came here because you were infatuated with Mme. d'Epernay. Well, I can afford to let you go; for, though my instincts cry out loudly for your death, I am a businessman, and I can suppress them when it has to be done. In brief, M. Hewlett, you can go when you choose.'

'M. Leroux,' I answered, 'I will say something to you for your own sake, and Mme. d'Epernay's, that I would not deign to say to any other man. She is as pure as the best woman in the land. I found her wandering in the street. I saved her from the assault of your hired ruffians. I tried to procure a room for her at the Merrimac, and when they refused her, I gave up my own apartment to her and went away.'

'But you went back!' he cried. 'You went back, Hewlett!'

'I can tell you no more,' I answered. 'Do you believe what I have said to you?'

He looked hard into my face. 'Yes,' he said simply. 'And it makes all the difference in the world to me.'

And at that moment, in spite of all, I felt no hatred toward the man. 'Père Antoine will marry you?' I asked.

'Yes,' he replied.

'And her father?'

'Is safe in the *château*, playing with his wheel and amassing a fortune in his dreams.'

'One word more,' I continued. 'Mme. d'Epernay is very ill. She was struck by one of those bullets that you fired through the door. Wait!' For he had started. 'I think that she will live. The wound cannot have pierced a vital part. But we must be very gentle in moving her. You had better bring the sleigh here, and you and I will lift her into it. And then — I shall not see her again.'

23

Leroux's *Diable*

I went back toward the cave. But I could not bring myself to see Jacqueline. Instead, I paced the tunnel to and fro, wondering what my life was going to be in future.

That I should love her till I died, I did not doubt at all.

Her last words had been in the nature of a final farewell. I must go before that old insatiable longing for her arose in me again.

I had reached the verge of the cataract and stood beside the little platform, looking down. There was no star now like that which had guided me in the morning, but the sky was fair and the air mild. I gazed in awe at the great stream of water, sending its ceaseless current down into the troubled lake below. How many ages it had done that! Yet even that must end someday, as everything ends — even life, thank God!

And then I saw Lacroix again. I was sure of it now. He was peering after me from among the rocks, and, as I turned, he was scuttling away into the tunnel. I followed him. I had always mistrusted the man; more, even, than Leroux. I felt that his furtive presence there portended something more evil than my own fate and Jacqueline's must be.

I followed him hotly; but he must have known every fissure in the cliff, for he vanished before my eyes, apparently through the solid rock, and when I reached the place of his disappearance I could find no sign of any passage there.

Well, there was no use in following him further. The sleigh ought to be at the mine in five minutes more. I turned back to take a last look at the cataract. The sublime grandeur of those thousand tons of water, shot from the glacier's edge above, still held me in its spell of awe. I cast my eyes toward the *château* and over the frozen lake toward the distant unknown mountains. Then I turned resolutely away.

And at that moment I heard Leroux's

voice hailing me, and looked round to see him emerge from the tunnel at my side. He was staring in bewilderment at the cataract.

'Hewlett, I don't know what possessed me to take the wrong turn tonight!' he cried. 'I have come through that tunnel a hundred times and never missed the path before.'

He swung round petulantly, and at that moment a shadow glided out of the darkness and stood in front of him. It was Pierre Caribou, lean, sinewy and old. He blocked the path and faced Leroux in silence.

Leroux looked at him, and an oath broke from his lips as he read the other's purpose upon his face. Squaring his mighty shoulders and clenching his fists, he leaped at him headlong.

Pierre stepped quietly aside, and Simon measured his full length within the tunnel. But when he had scrambled to his feet with a bellowing challenge, Pierre was in front of him again.

'What are you here for?' roared Leroux, but in a quavering voice that did not sound like his own. 'Get out of the way or I'll smash your face!'

The Indian still blocked the passage. 'Your time has come now, Simon. All finished now,' he answered.

Simon drew back a pace and watched him, breathing hard.

'You came here one, two years ago,' Pierre continued. 'You ate up the home of M. Duchaine, my master. I belong here. You ate up everything, came back, ate up some more. Then you sold Mlle. Jacqueline to Louis d'Epernay. You made her run away to New York. I asked your *diable* when your time would come. Your *diable* said wait. I waited. Mlle. Jacqueline came back. I asked your *diable* again. He said wait some more. Now your *diable* has told me he sent you here tonight because your time had come.'

The face that Simon turned on me was that of a hopeless man who knows that everything he had prized is lost. He cowered now before Pierre Caribou. 'Hewlett!' he cried in a quavering voice. 'Help me throw this old fool out of the way.'

I spoke to Pierre, 'Our quarrel is at an end. I am going away. You must go, too.'

Pierre Caribou did not relax an inch of ground. Then a roar burst from Leroux's lips, and he flung himself upon the Indian in the same desperate way as I had experienced, and in an instant the two men were struggling at the edge of the platform. It was impossible for me to intervene, and I could only stand by and stare in horror. And, as I stared, I saw the face of Lacroix among the rocks again, peering out with an evil smile upon his lips.

Whether they fought in silence or whether in sound I do not know, for the noise of the cataract rendered the battle a dumb pantomime. Pierre had pulled the Frenchman out to the middle of the ledge and was trying to force him over. But Leroux was clinging with one hand to the cliff and with the other he beat savagely upon his enemy's face, so that the blood covered both of them. But Pierre did not seem to feel the blows.

Leroux, one-handed, was at a disadvantage. He grasped his antagonist again, and the death-grapple began. It was a marvel that they could engage in so terrific a fight upon the ice-coated ledge and hold their balance there. But I saw that they were in equipoise, for they were bending all the tension of each muscle to the fight, so that they remained almost motionless, and, thigh to thigh, arm to arm, breast to breast, each sought to break the other's strength. And I saw that, when one was broken, he would not yield slowly, but, having spent the last of his strength, would collapse like a crumpled cardboard figure and go down into the boiling lake.

The cataract's half-sphere of crystal clearness framed them as though they formed some dreadful picture. They bent and swayed, and now Leroux was forcing Pierre's head and shoulders backward by the weight of his bull's body. But the Indian's sinews, toughened by years of toil to steel, held fast; and just as Leroux, confident of victory, shifted his feet and inclined forward, Pierre changed his grasp and caught him by the throat.

Leroux's face blackened and his eyes

started out. His great chest heaved, and he tore impotently at his enemy's strong fingers that were shutting out air and light and consciousness. They rocked and swayed; then, with a last convulsive effort, Leroux swung Pierre off his feet, raised him high in the air, and tried to dash his body against the projecting rock at the tunnel's mouth.

But still the Indian's fingers held, and as his consciousness began to fade Leroux staggered and slipped; and with a neighing whine that burst from his constricted throat, a shriek that pierced the torrent's roar, he slid down the cataract, Pierre locked in his arms.

I cried out in horror, but leaned forward, fascinated by the dreadful spectacle. I saw the bodies glide down the straight jet of water, as a boy might slide down a column of steel, and plunge into the black cauldron beneath, around whose edge stood the mocking and fantastic figures of ice. The seething lake tossed them high into the air, and the second cataract caught them and flung them back toward the Old Angel.

Their waters played with them and spun them round, caught them, and let them go, and roared and foamed about them as they bobbed and danced their devil's jig, waist-high, in one another's arms. At last they slid down into the depths of the dark lake, to lie forever there in that embrace. And still the cataracts played on, sounding their loud, triumphant, never-ending tune. I was running down the tunnel again.

I was running to Jacqueline, but something diverted me. It was the face of Lacroix, peering at me from among the crevices of the rocks with the same evil smile. I knew from the look on it that he had seen all and had been infinitely pleased thereby. I caught at him; I wanted to get my hands on him and strangle him, too, and fling him down, and stamp his features out of human semblance. But he eluded me and darted back into the cliff.

I followed him hard. This time I did not mean to let him go.

Lacroix was running toward the gold mine. He made no effort to dodge into any of the unknown recesses of the caves, but ran at full speed across the open space and plunged into the tunnel leading to the shore by the *château*.

I caught him near the entrance and held him fast. He struggled in my grasp and screamed: 'Go back! For the love of God, go back, *monsieur*! Let me go! Let me go!'

He slipped out of my hands and darted into the mine again, taking the tunnel which led toward the Old Angel, and thence wound back toward the *château*. I caught him again before the cave where Jacqueline lay. I wound my arms around him. A dreadful suspicion was creeping into my mind. He made no attempt to fight me, but only to escape, and his face was hideously stamped with fear.

'Let me go!' he howled. 'I will give you a half-share in the gold. What do you want with me?'

What did I want? I did not know. It must have been the same instinct that leads one to stamp upon a noxious insect. I think it was his joy in the hideous spectacle beneath the cataract that had made me long to kill him. But now a dreadful fear was dawning on me.

'Jacqueline!' I screamed.

'I have not seen her,' he replied. 'Now let me go! Ah, *mon Dieu*, it is too late!' Suddenly he grew calm. 'It is too late,' he said in a monotonous voice. 'You have killed both of us!' And, with the sweat still on his forehead, he stood looking maliciously at me.

I saw the face of the cliff quiver; I saw an immense rock, halfway up, leap into the air and seem to hang there; then the ground was upheaved beneath my feet, and with a frightful roar the rocky walls swayed and fell together.

And the rivulet became a cataract that surged over me and filled my ears with tumult and sealed my eyes with sleep.

24

Full Confession

Darkness impenetrable about me, and a thick air that I breathed with great gasps that hardly brought relief to my choking throat. And a voice out of the darkness crying ceaselessly in my ears: '*Help me! Help me!*'

In that nightmare I saw again those awful scenes. I saw the last struggle of Pierre and Leroux, and I pursued Lacroix along the tunnel. I saw the cliff toppling forward, and the rock poised in mid-air. And the voice cried: 'Help me! *Help me!*' and never ceased.

I raised myself and tried to struggle to my feet. I found that I could move my limbs freely. I tried to rise upon my knees, but the roof struck my head. I stretched my arms out, and I touched the wall on either side of me. I must have been stunned by the concussion of the landslide. By a miracle I had not been struck.

I tried to find the voice. I crawled three feet toward it, and the wall stopped me. But the voice was there. It came from under the wall. I felt about me in the darkness, and my hand touched something damp. I whipped it back in horror. It was the face of a man.

There was only the face. Where the body and limbs ought to have been was only rock. The face was on my side of a wall of rock, pinning down the body that lay outstretched beyond. I recognized the voice now. It was that of Philippe Lacroix.

'Ah, *mon Dieu*! Help me! Help me!'

He continued to repeat the words in every conceivable tone, and his suffering was pitiable. I forgot my own troubles as I tried to aid him. All my efforts were vain. There were tons of rock above him, and under the inch or two of space where the rock rested above the ground I felt the edge of a burlap bag.

He had been pinned beneath the bags of earth and gold which he had prized so dearly; the golden rocks were grinding out his life. He was dying — and he could not take his treasures to that place to which he must go. I felt one hand come through the tiny opening in the wall and grasp at me.

'Who is it?' he mumbled. 'Is that you, Hewlett? For God's sake, kill me!'

I crouched beside him, but I did not know what to say or do. I could only wait there, that he might not die alone.

'Give me a knife!' he mumbled again, clutching at me. 'A knife, Hewlett! Don't leave me to die like this! Bring Père Antoine and my mother. I want to tell her — to tell her — '

He muttered in his delirium until his voice died away. I thought that he would never speak again. But presently he seemed to revive again to the consciousness of his surroundings.

'Are you with me, Hewlett?' he whispered. I placed my hand in his, and he clutched at it with feverish force. 'You will have the gold, Hewlett,' he muttered, apparently ignorant that I, too, was a prisoner and in hardly better plight. 'You are the last of the four. I tried to kill you, Hewlett.'

I said nothing, and he repeated

querulously, between his gasps: 'I tried to kill you, Hewlett. Are you going to leave me to die alone in the dark now?'

'No,' I answered. 'It doesn't matter, Lacroix.' And, really, it did not matter.

'I wanted to kill you,' his voice rambled on. 'Leroux is dead. I watched him die. I thought if you died, too, no one but I would know the secret of the gold. I tried to murder you. I blew up the tunnel!'

He paused a while, and again I thought he was dying, but once more he took up the confession.

'There was nearly a quarter of a ton of blasting powder and dynamite in the cave. You didn't know. You went about so blindly, Hewlett. I watched you when I talked with you that night here. How long ago it must have been! When was that?'

I did not tell him it was yesterday. For it seemed immeasurably long ago to me as well.

'It was stored there,' he said. 'We had brought it up from St. Boniface by sleigh — so carefully. Leroux intended to begin mining as soon as Louis returned. And when he died I meant to kill you both, so that the gold should all be mine. I told you it was here because I thought you meant to kill me, but I meant to kill you when you had made an end of Leroux. And you killed me. Damn you!' he snarled. 'Why did you not let me go?'

He paused, and I heard him gasp for breath. His fingers clutched at my coat sleeve again and hooped themselves round mine like claws of steel.

'I had a knife — once,' he resumed, relapsing into his delirium, 'but I left it behind me and the police got it. Isn't it odd, Leroux,' he rambled on, 'that one always leaves something behind when one has killed a man? But the newspapers made no mention about the knife. You didn't know he was dead, did you, Leroux, for all your cleverness, until that fool Hewlett left that paper upon the table? You knew enough to send me to jail, but you didn't know that it was I who killed him. Help me!' He screamed horribly. 'He is here, looking at me!'

'There is nobody here, Philippe,' I said, trying to soothe his agony of soul. What a poor and stained soul it was, travelling into the next world alone! 'There is nobody but me, Philippe!'

'You lie!' he raved. 'Louis is here! He has come for me! Give me your knife, Hewlett. It is for him, not for me. He deserved to die. He tricked me after we had found the gold. He tricked me twice. He told Leroux, thinking that he would win his gratitude and get free from the man's power. And the second time he told Carson.'

My heart was thumping as he spoke. I hardly dared to hope his words were true.

'He was my friend,' he mumbled. 'We were friends since we were boys. We would have kicked Leroux into the street if he had dared to enter our homes. But we owed so much money. And he discovered — what we had done. He wanted our family interest; he wanted to make use of us. And when we found the mine, Louis thought we would never be in need of money again. But Leroux was pressing him, threatening him. And so he told him. Then there were three of us in the secret.

'Leroux had formed a lumber company with Carson, but he did not tell him about the gold. He formed his scheme with Louis. They said nothing to me; they wanted to leave me out. Louis was to get the woman and sell his rights to Simon. But afterward, when he had spent the money Simon had given him, he thought he could get more out of Carson. So he went to him and told the secret. That made four of us — four of us, where there should have been only two.'

'What did you do?' I asked, though it was like conducting a post-mortem upon a murderer's corpse.

'I went to New York to get my share. I wasn't going to be ousted, I, who had been one of the discoverers. I don't know how much Carson paid Louis, but I meant to demand half. I thought he had the money in his pocket.

'I followed him all that afternoon after he had left Carson's office. I watched him in the street. At night he went to a room somewhere — at the top of a tall building. I followed him. When I got in I found a woman there. Louis was talking to her and threatening her. He said she was his wife. How could she be his wife when he had married Jacqueline Duchaine?

'I didn't care — it was no business of mine. I couldn't see them, because there was a curtain in the way. There was no light in the bedroom. There was a light in the room in which I was. I put it out, so that neither of them should see my face. She might have betrayed me, you know, Simon.

'He spun round when the light went out, and pushed the curtain aside. I was waiting for that. I had calculated my blow. I stabbed him. It was a good blow, though it was delivered in the dark. He only cried out once. But the woman screamed, and a dog flew at me, and I couldn't find his money. So I ran away.

'And then there were only three of us who knew the secret. Then Simon died and there were only two, and now there are only Hewlett and I, and he is dead, poor fool, and I have my gold here. For God's sake give me a knife, Simon!'

His fingers tore at my sleeve in his last agony, and I was tempted sorely. And it was his own knife that I had. The irony of it!

He muttered once or twice and cried

out in fear of the man whom he had slain. I heard him gasp a little later. Then the hand fell from my sleeve. And after that there was no further sound . . .

'Paul?'

It was the merest whisper from the wall. I thought it was a trick of my own mind. I dared not hope.

'Paul! Dearest!'

This was no fancy born of a delirious brain and the thick fumes of dynamite. It came from the wall a little way ahead of me. I crawled the three feet that the little cave afforded and put my hands upon the rock, feeling its surface inch by inch. There was a crevice there, not large enough to have permitted a bird to pass — the merest fissure.

'Jacqueline! Is that you?' I called.

'Where are you, Paul?' she whispered back.

'Behind the wall,' I answered. 'You are not hurt?'

'I am lying where you left me, dear. I — I heard.'

'You heard?' I answered dully. What did it matter now?

'Why didn't you tell me, Paul? But never mind. Can you come through to me?'

I struggled to tear the rocks away; I beat and bruised my hands in vain against them.

'Soon,' I muttered. 'Soon. Can you breathe well?'

'It is all open, Paul. It is nearly dawn now.'

'I will come when it grows light,' I babbled. 'When it grows light!'

She did not know that it would never grow light for me. Again I flung myself against the walls of my prison, battering at them till the blood dripped from my hands. Again and again I flung myself down hopelessly, and then I tried again, clutching at every fragment that pro-truded into the cave.

And at last, when my despair had mastered me — it grew light. For a sunbeam shot like a finger through the crevice and quivered upon the floor of the cave. And overhead, where I had never thought to seek, where I had thought three hundred feet of eternal rock pressed down on me, I saw the quiver of day through half a dozen feet of tight-packed debris from the glacier's mouth.

I raised myself and tore at it and sent it flying. I thrust my hands among the stones and tore them down like the tiles from a rotten roof. I heard a shout; hands were reached down to me and pulled me up, and I was on my feet upon a hillside, looking into the keen eyes of Père Antoine and the face of the Indian squaw.

And the husky dog was barking at my side.

25

The End of the Château

Only one thing marred the happiness of our reunion, and that was the loss of Jacqueline's father. We had talked much over what had happened, and ten days later, when Jacqueline had recovered from the shock and from what proved to be, after all, only a flesh wound, we had visited the scene of our rescue by the old priest.

The Indian woman had met him as she was returning home, and had told him of our danger, and he had started out before dawn, to find that there was no longer any entrance to the tunnel. Wandering in bewilderment upon the mountains, he had reached the place where I was buried at the moment of my final effort to break through the debris overhead. Although the explanation seemed an impossible one, there was none other. The cliff, riddled with tunnels and eaten out by its numerous subterranean streams, had fallen. The charge of dynamite exploded, as it happened, beneath that part which buttressed the entire structure, combining with the pressure of the glacier above, had thrown the mountain on its side, filling the lake with several million tons of ice and obliterating all traces of the *château*, which lay buried beneath its waters. That was Père Antoine's explanation, and we realized at once that it was useless to search for Charles Duchaine. The whole aspect of the region had been changed; there was neither glacier nor cataract, and the lake, swollen to twice its size and height, slept peacefully beneath its covering of ice and snow.

When we returned to the cabin, we were amazed to see a sleigh standing outside, and dogs feeding. Two men were seated at the priest's table, smoking.

'*Diable, monsieur*, don't you keep a stove in your house?' shouted a well-known voice to Père Antoine. Then, as Jacqueline and I approached the entrance, the man turned and sprang toward us with outstretched hands that gripped ours and wrung them till we cried out in pain. It was Alfred Dubois.

But I was stupefied to see the second man who rose and advanced toward me with a shrewd smile. For it was Tom Carson!

Presently I was telling my story — except for that part which more intimately concerned myself and Jacqueline, and the narrative of the murder, which I gave only as Lacroix had confessed it to me.

A look of incredulity deepened on Tom's shrewd old face till, at the end, he burst out explosively at me: 'Hewlett, I didn't think I was a damned fool before — I beg your pardon, miss. If any man had told me that I would have knocked him down. But I am, I am, and want you to be my manager.'

'Do you mean that I have lied to you?' I asked indignantly.

'Every word, Hewlett — every word, my son. That is why I want you back with me. First you leave my employment without offering any reason; then you take hold of my business affairs and try to pull off a deal over my head, and then you tell me a yarn about a castle falling into a lake.'

'But, M. Carson,' interposed the priest, 'I myself have seen this *château* many times. And I have gone to the entrance and looked from the mountain, too, and it is no longer there.'

'Never was,' said Carson. 'You fellows get so lonesome up in these wilds that you have to see things.'

'But I heard the explosion.'

'Artillery practice down the Gulf.'

'Listen to me, M. Carson!' exploded Dubois. 'Did I not say that I would drive you here myself because I was anxious about a friend of mine and his young bride who were in the clutches of that scoundrel, Simon Leroux, who killed my brother? And did I not say that they were in the *Château* Duchaine?'

'Well, there may be a *château* somewhere,' Carson replied. 'In fact, there probably is. This man, d'Epernay, who is said to be dead now, wanted to sell me the biggest gold mine in the world for fifty thousand dollars, and from what I know of Leroux I am ready to believe that he would try to hog it if it really exists. So, as I wanted to see how our lumber development at St. Boniface was getting along, I thought I'd come up here and investigate.'

'But how about Leroux?' I cried, more amused now than vexed.

'That,' answered Tom, 'is precisely why I want to get hold of you again, Mr. Hewlett.'

'But *here* is Mlle. Duchaine!' shouted the old priest in despair.

Tom Carson raised his fat old body about five inches and made Jacqueline what he took to be a bow. 'Pleased to make your acquaintance, miss,' he replied. 'Ah, well, it doesn't matter. I guess that man, d'Epernay, was lying to me. He wanted to get a cash advance, and I got a little suspicious of him just about then. However, I am ready to look at your gold mine if you want me to.'

'You'll have to do some blasting then,' I said, nettled. 'It's just about two hundred feet below the ground.'

'Never mind,' said Tom. 'Lumber is

better than gold. Next time I'm here I shall be glad to have another look around. And now, Hewlett, if you want a job at five thousand a year to start — to start, mind you, you play fair and tell me where Leroux is hiding — '

I was too mortified to answer him. But I felt Jacqueline slip her hand into mine, and suddenly the memory of the past made Tom's raillery an insignificant affair.

'Mind you,' he pursued, 'he'll turn up soon. He's got to turn up, because the lumber company's all organized now and in fine running order. What do you say, Hewlett?'

'Nothing,' I answered.

'All right,' he said, turning away with a shrug of his shoulders. 'Unpractical as ever, ain't you? Think it over, my son. Glad to have met you, Mr. Priest, and as I'm always busy I guess Dubois and I will start for home this afternoon.'

Jacqueline looked at me, and I shook my head. I didn't want Tom to witness it. But a word from Père Antoine changed the hostile tenor of my thoughts to warm and human ones.

'*Messieurs*,' he said, 'doubtless you know what day this is?'

Tom started. 'Why, good Lord, it — it's Christmas Day, isn't it?' he asked, a little sheepishly.

'It's a bigger day for us,' I said to Tom.

He squinted at me in his shrewd manner; and then he got up from the table and wrung my hand.

'Good luck to you both,' he said. 'Say, Mr. Dubois, I guess we can pitch our tent here tonight — don't you?'